SPACE RENEGADES

By

Paul R Starling

Copyright
Paul R Starling
Contact: p.starling@sky.com

Front cover artwork
Chloe Starling

This Edition 2025

All rights reserved. No part of this publication may be reproduced, stored in a retrieval system, or transmitted in any form or by any means, electronic, mechanical, photocopy, recording or otherwise, without prior written permission from the copyright holder. Nor can it be circulated in any form of binding or cover other than that in which it is published and without similar condition being imposed on a similar purchaser.

Any mention of Star Trek is obviously not my own copyright. That belongs to Paramount Pictures!

For
Mac and Bernard

Introduction

Space Renegades was originally conceived by myself and written between 1985 and 1988. These ninety-three very short stories were my homage/ripoff of the two "Star" franchises: "Wars" and "Trek". But mostly inspired by the latter. I was a fan of the adventures of Captain James T. Kirk and the crew aboard the Starship Enterprise, following them in their television adventures - repeats/reruns, of course, because I wasn't born until 1971! - and the early movies, especially the fourth film, which I saw twice at the cinema on its release, my first ever multiple theatrical view of a film, fact fans!

Once I finished with the short-stories, I wrote a novel featuring the main characters from Space Renegades, which used a few of the shorter story plot points but with an overreaching arc.

In 1987 my "Trek" fandom increased with the release of Star Trek The Next Generation. I repeatedly watched the pilot episode on VHS tape - I was very fortunate enough to work in a video library at the time of its release - plus the subsequent two episodes on the same format, but it wasn't until I persuaded my parents that we desperately needed a Sky Television subscription, that I was able to follow this particular crew throughout their entire run of adventures.

I was hooked!

I became an everlasting fan!

Incidentally, the ship in my stories was called Bucktoo but, for this version and in homage to Exel

Electrical store/video library where I worked back in the day, I have renamed the vessel: Sol Ship Excel.

The following stories in their original format were conceived as basic scripts, and not as detailed and fully fleshed short-stories. I would read these scripts to a friend who was also a Star Trek fan, and some were even recorded onto cassette tape via a very rudimentary shoe-box recorder with sound effects…one might say in modern parlance it was a fan fiction/podcast rolled into one!

While trying my best to adhere to this original concept in this new collection of stories based upon those original Space Renegade scripts, and whilst also maintaining much of their 1980's integrity as best I can, I have inevitably updated them for myriad reasons. Like many things from our past which now appear very dated in their depiction of various stereotypes, these would definitely fail several modern "appropriateness" and "problematic"tests! So my dilemma was: what to keep, what to take away, and what to add? Am I precious about my original artistic vision? Am I pretentious enough to believe I had any artistic vision to begin with, or now, for that matter?

And my answer was…not especially!

While adapting these stories for this collection I discovered that it has been many years - perhaps decades? - since I last read through them and as a consequence, as well as the numerous faults and feelings they aren't as terrible as I recalled, I came to wonder why these space travellers were actually 'Renegades.' This was a question I seemingly failed to address or answer at their first writing, back in the

80's. Maybe that small detail it didn't really matter back then, maybe they were 'Renegades' simply because I liked the word! Who knows? But at least now I have answered that question by adding a bit of meaning, however tangential, to these stories.

EPISODE ONE

(Original script 25th May 1985)

'ERSATZ'

The village on planet Uraskus Prime shouldn't be there. Ships sensors have detected no signs of a civilisation whatsoever. The landing party with their hand-held scanners have detect no structures whatsoever. Yet their eyes do not deceive them.

It's almost as if a section of a rural English village from the nineteen-eighties has been removed from Earth and transplanted in the middle of this sun-bleached, mountainous landscape, millions of miles from its rightful location.

"Not only is the village utterly incongruous, it cannot be real!" It is Commander Ariana Mocha who speaks first, not because of her accepted seniority in rank, but because it is an annoying habit she possesses , to trample over anybody else's words until they are stopped and forced to listen.

Commander Mocha checks the readout on the touch screen of her handheld scanner, performing a full perimeter sweep of the area, and besides the three of them and their shuttlecraft, the scanner confirms there is nothing but a lifeless, barren wasteland in front of and all around them.

"Commander!" Lieutenant Z'Dar says via his implanted voice translator - this particular crew member of the Sol Ship Excel is not originally from planet Earth. "This makes no sense!"

"What makes no sense?"

"My scanner shows one life-form two-hundred yards ahead…"

"…From within the village which shouldn't exist!?"

Doctor Kelly D, the third member of the shuttle crew, looks befuddled as she scans the same region, "Nothing on mine, Lieutenant! You must have a faulty scanner."

"Let's investigate." Commander Mocha suggests.

"Genius!" Doctor Kelly D says.

The Sol Ship Excel landing party enter the outskirts of the village which isn't there. Sand and rock turns abruptly to tarmac road beneath their feet. Bungalows and chalets are set behind flowered and grassed garden spaces, with pathways leading to front doors on either side. Signage declares this to be Waveney Close, the road wending its way forward in zigzagging curves. It's almost as if…

"It's almost as if," Commander Mocha jumps in, "this is one of those historic holograms back on Earth."

"But where are the…" Lieutenant Z'Dar begins to say.

"Where are the people?" Mocha interrupts as if no hearing anyone else!

Doctor D mutters: "Give the Lieutenant a chance to speak."

"What was that, Doctor?" Mocha asks.

"With all due respects, Commander." Doctor Kelly D says. "But as you know, your habit of butting in and talking over people is…"

"Annoying?"

"Exactly!"

"Sorry, Doctor. I shall make no attempt to alter my personality based upon your astute professional recommendation. I am what I am!"

"Analysis, people!" The voice of Captain Xero Cirroc emanates loudly from the trio's communication pads on their shoulders - a device approximately half the size of twenty-first century mobile phones, just so you know - and causes Lieutenant Z'Dar to visibly jump.

Doctor Kelly D says, "Ariana's being her usual annoying self, Captain!"

Commander Mocha pouts.

Captain Cirroc chuckles. "Anything unusual?"

"Captain." Lieutenant Z'Dar says, sighing lovingly, his voice out of sync with his mouth. "We are now walking through a village similar to some of those on your Earth's Historical Database. My scanner also shows one life-form energy reading near our position."

There's a brief delay before Captain Cirroc responds. "Ships scanners show only the three of you and the shuttlecraft down there. And that you should presently be walking amidst a barren, sun-bleached mountainous wasteland."

"Confirmed, Captain." Commander Mocha says. "Our sensors offer identical information to that of the ship, and yet we are most assuredly walking along a tarmac road in what appears to be a suburban environment."

"Okay." Captain Cirroc's voice resonates with thoughtful consideration. "Keep me informed, and proceed with caution!"

Doctor Kelly D mutters: "As if we'd do anything else!"

"What was that, Doctor.?"

"Nothing, Captain."

"Oh, okay. Cirroc out!"

The trio keep a steady pace along the road, observing as they go, moving ever nearer to the life-form showing only upon Lieutenant Z'Dar's hand-held scanner. The scene around them is unchanged. Suburban homes with a woodland abutting their rear, neat frontages, well maintained gardens and no moving objects except for the three Sol Ship Excel crew members.

"How do you suppose this illusion is created, Commander?" Z'Dar asks with one eye on the scanner in his hand.

"I'm not sure." Mocha answers honestly. "Without any readings from any obvious electronic devices we can only assume this isn't a projection hologram. Of course, this being an alien planet, we don't know if our technology would be able to detect theirs. Especially if theirs is more sophisticated, which I hypothesis is very likely to be the case, based on what our eyes are seeing. . Maybe the life-sign energy reading on your scanner belongs to a higher form of sentience, which will be able to communicate with us, and thus explain everything that we need to know. Also, it might be able to show us to the source of the thing we are here to collect for our Chief Engineer."

"Well, duh!" Doctor Kelly D mutters under her breath - she mutters a lot!

On the bridge of the Sol Ship Excel, Captain Xero Cirroc paces back and forth, forth and back, between Chief Engineer Mathilde Scobryne and the helm, personed by Lieutenant Commander Chiwetel Jones.

"Captain!" Engineer Scobryne pipes up.
"That's right!" Captain Cirroc replies.
"I'm detecting an energy build-up on the surface of the planet!"
"What's it building, Chief?"
"It's increasing in size, sir. Strewth…it's huge!"
"Huge! How huge?"
"Huge, sir."
"But how huge?"
"Huge!"
"On screen!"
"Er, no, sir…on the planet!"

Captain Cirroc sighs patiently. "Jones." The helmsman turns in his seat to face the Captain, his expression nervous. "Can you put the planet on the viewing screen for me please?…and, also, if it's not too much trouble, can you also display for me the energy reading?"

Lieutenant Commander Jones sighs with relief - he thought he was in trouble - nods, and does as instructed. The blue and green planet Uraskus Prime looms large on the viewing screen. An overlaid pixelated red glow, rapidly increasing in mass, throbs menacingly on the upper-right section.

"It's getting nearer." Jones states the obvious, the panic rising in his voice. "And it's on an intercept course!"

"Confirmed." Confirms Scobryne.

"Move us away, Jones." The Captain calmly orders. "Steady as she goes."

"Aye, Captain." Jones replies, on the brink of tears.

The image of Uraskus Prime recedes on the viewing screen but the pixelated dot of energy increases in speed and size.

"I've got a bad feeling…" The Captain is cut off - thankfully! - when the pulsating red energy glow fully engulfs the Sol Ship Excel.

An automated alert klaxon blares. The ship shudders briefly before its inertia stabilisers correct the inertia. The red glow has vanished.

"Intruder alert!" Announces the electronic voice of the shipboard commuter HEAL - which stands for Holographically Emitted Artificial Life-form.

Captain Cirroc sits down at a console beside Chief Engineer Scobryne, who adjusts her hair. He studies the technobabble readouts which are pretty much gobbledygook to him.

"Status?" He asks Scobryne.

"Still single, sir." The Chief replies flirtatiously.

"Status of our ship, Lieutenant."

"I know. Well, the ship is fine…but like HEAL just said, we do have an intruder onboard." She pulls up a visual display on the screen at her station, which even the Captain can understand, and looks lovingly at him. "The energy pattern has coalesced into an approximation of humanoid size and it's on its way to the bridge, Captain."

"Oh…no!" Says Lieutenant Commander Chiwetel Jones, knuckles at his mouth, terrified.

The Captain thinks nothing of the Lieutenants reaction because this isn't exactly their first rodeo! He taps the communication device attached to the shoulder pad of his uniform: "Captain to landing party. We've encountered an energy form directed at us from the planet. At the moment it presents no threat. What's your status."

"Still single, Captain," comes the reply from Commander Mocha, "but open to offers!"

"Never gets old!"

"No change here, Captain, but I…"

"Thank you, Commander. Cirroc out."

"Nicely done, sir." The Chief Engineer says.

"You know how she rambles on! Can we get a couple of security officers up here just in case our guest becomes hostile?"

"Doesn't that seem a bit superfluous, Captain?" Asks the Chief. "I mean…a being with enough energy to do what it's just done won't exactly be concerned by a couple of burly, eye-candy, security officers."

"Quite right, Chief. I was just testing!"

On the planet Uraskus Prime, halfway along Waveney Close, the Sol Ship Excel's landing party have stopped, and not to admire the delightful view. Lieutenant Z'Dar is pointing at a building which is set back from the houses. This building, set back and along a gravel driveway, is incongruous among the homes.

"The life-form is this way." Lieutenant Z'Dar states tremulously, pointing along the gravel driveway.

"A library?" Doctor Kelly D notes the word which is etched into the red brick frontage above the double-doors of the building, it's three-storey visage is an incongruity within an anomaly - yeah!

"What is a library?" Lieutenant Z'Dar asks innocently. "I am only familiar with the library of files onboard our ship, and similar on Earth. This looks nothing like the library I am familiar with."

"It used to be a repository for books." Doctor Kelly D tells him. "On Earth, now, these books are stored in our preservation Museums located across the globe. I guess this must be what libraries used to look like."

Unusually, Commander Mocha remains silent.

The trio enter the austere building by pushing open the front doors - as you do, but they normally don't! - and the cavernous, gaping, musty library interior is empty. No books, no furniture, just empty space with walls lined with shelves. A solid wooden staircase wends up to a balcony which sides all four of the walls, where books should be but there are none.

Two doors are located either side of the foot of the staircase.

"The energy life form is through…" Lieutenant Z'Dar starts but doesn't finish.

"What…" Doctor D says but…

"What is it, Lieutenant." Commander Mocha prompts.

"The energy signs…"

"Have gone." Mocha finishes. "As have the books in this library, it appears! But not the shelves for them. I suggest we try both the doors at the back there?"

Doctor D mutters: "Why don't you let someone complete…"

"…their sentences, doctor!?"

"That's right!"

Commander Mocha leads them through the big empty room, oblivious to the effects of her own attitude, and she isn't even an alien! When she opens the first door the room is impossibly large.

"This building is bigger on the inside than out." The Commander states. "And my scanner doesn't show anything at all. It senses no make!"

"What are these things?" Lieutenant Z'Dar asks.

"They look like…magazines!?" Doctor Kelly D says with curiosity.

The abnormally large room is filled with stacks of slim volumes of magazine sized magazines on all four sides, from floor to ceiling, with ample room between to move around.

"What are…magazines?" The Lieutenant asks innocently.

"I believe magazines were disposable paper based publications," Commander Mocha explains, "popular on Earth until the mid-twenty-first century when deforestation was widespread and rationing began. Like books, they ceased producing paper based articles to save the planet! We were once a wasteful, greedy and destructive civilisation, and naive back in the bad old days. Magazines were called…periodicals, I believe. They varied from general human interests, entertainment, machines, and…" she pulls out one of the magazines from a stack, "…comic books!?"

Lieutenant Z'Dar and Doctor D look on with fascination at the brightly coloured cover, with it's flimsy paper and garish design.

"Bee…Nee!" The Lieutenant pronounces at length. "What does it…mean? What is a…comic book?"

"I'm not entirely sure." Commander Mocha tells the young Lieutenant. "But it appears these lurid and childlike images are most probably hand drawn, while the text itself appears to be printed, but I suspect it too is made by someone rather than a machine."

"Look at the date." Doctor Kelly D says. "Twenty-eighth of…

"…September, ninety eight-five!" Commander Mocha finishes. "Issue number one! I cannot see any significance whatsoever in this date!"

"That's over three-hundred years ago!" Doctor Kelly D states for no reason other than to let us know the current time frame via some very vital exposition - well done, Doctor!

Once Commander Mocha fans through the equally colourful and vibrantly rendered pages of the comic book, Lieutenant Z'Dar picks up another from one of the stacks. He looks at it with childlike awe, reading every word upon the cover, absorbing the artwork. Z'Dar fans through it slowly, deliberately, his sophisticated electronic contact lenses performing their necessary visual translation, informing him about the characters and stories offered within this particular publication.

"Nothing like this exists on my planet!" Z'Dar states with obvious wonder in his voice. "This...comic is dated September twenty-eighth...twenty fifty-one. Issue two-thousand six hundred!"

"It seems these...comics," Doctor D offers, "represent an artistic approach to storytelling?"

"Can we take them back to the ship?" Z'Dar asks with excited hope in his voice.

His colleagues regard him skeptically, saying nothing, just looking upon the staggering entirety of this collection, both wordlessly wondering how long it would take to carry them to their shuttle craft.

"Hmmm." Says Commander Mocha, thoughtfully stroking her beard. "What does all this mean? Firstly, we have a village which isn't here. Then a disappearing life form! Now, an empty library with an impossibly large interior. And comic books with an Earth origin. Who could have put these here? And most importantly...why?"

On the bridge of Sol Ship Excel the crew are faced with a shape-shifting, humanoid-size free floating energy form. It changes colour in rainbow rotation and glides across the rectangular bridge, going from person to person, console to console until stopping directly in front of the large forward-facing viewing screen. The crew cannot tell if it's looking at them or at its planet of origin, or neither.

"Uh...hello." Captain Cirroc hesitantly says. "Welcome to my...that is...the Sol Ship Excel. I'm Captain Xero Cirroc."

The energy form oscillates, gradually coalescing into a more readily identifiable form...that of a humanoid approximation, but translucent, while the uniform, skin and hair form a single smooth layer.

"My name," it announces, the voice closely resembling the pitch of the Captain's in its attempt to acceptably mimic what it hears as normal, "is Triandos! My planet is...there." It's floating apparition for an arm extends towards the planet Uraskus Prime.

"Uraskus Prime." Captain Cirroc says.

"That is...the name you use for it. Your... computer...not easy for me. I...need your... assistance."

The translucent humanoid form shifts into a smaller shape, breaks apart with a pulsating ball of light, before reforming once more, but now the hair resembles that of Chief Engineer Scobryne and the uniform has turned into a fully formed human skin.

"I...cannot hold your human form." Triandos explains.

"I think you look beautiful." Scobryne says, admiring the approximation of her naked self.

"I'm scared!" Announces Lieutenant Commander Jones from his position at helm control, covering his eyes.

"How can we offer our assistance, Triandos?" Captain Cirroc asks heroically.

A uniform shimmers into existence over the naked form, changing colours with regularity.

"There is…danger. We must leave here. Triandos has…a…a…?"

"Brother?" Captain Cirroc ventures. "Sister?"

"Lover?" Suggests Scobryne.

"D…d…doppelgänger!?" Jones whimpers from his seat at the helm.

"Prisoner. On… Uraskus Prime." Triandos says. Its humanoid form shimmers to an effervescence state of being, floating above the bridge deck like a ghosts, if ghosts were real, which controversially they're not.

The words 'a dangerous prisoner' form magically, only magic isn't real either, like ghosts, upon the viewing screen.

Captain Cirroc taps his shoulder communicator - which is real, obviously, "Cirroc to landing party!"

The first to respond is Doctor Kelly D, "Not my idea of a party, Captain!"

"What's happening down there?"

The trio on Uraskus Prime have moved out of the comic book room into the main library, which is still devoid of books, although the life form reading on Lieutenant Z'Dar's hand-held scanner has returned, indicating that whatever it was has now gone outside the building .

"The life form had initially disappeared, Captain." Explains Commander Mocha. "But has reappeared outside. The building itself, which we tracked the life-form to, was a library although it's internal dimensions are curiously larger than its external dimensions! Also, there are no books or furniture within, just shelves, a staircase and doors, all of which we tried, leading into empty rooms except one, in which we found some...magazines."

"Technically it was the first room!" Doctor D adds. "And it was some comic books!"

"We've got our own energy being up here!" Captain Xero Cirroc says, and fills in some exposition for the Uraskus Prime landing party. "It seems benevolent enough...but it claims there's a dangerous criminal on the surface."

"We found some...comic books, Captain?" Doctor Kelly D adds something else!

"Can we bring some back, Captain?" Lieutenant Z'Dar shouts excitedly.

"What are..." Captain Cirroc's voice asks, "...comic books."

"They're these..." Z'Dar starts.

"They're not important right now!" Commander Mocha interrupts. "The important thing is, Captain...that the life form which has now reappeared outside is on our agenda."

"Acknowledged, Commander, be..." The Captain's transmission is cut off.

"Yes, Captain? Be...what?" Commander Mocha taps her shoulder communication device. "Be what, Captain?"

"Good grief, Commander," Doctor Kelly D says, "can't you tell when communications have been cut off? How many times have we done this!? I suggest we leave...because that's probably what Captain Cirroc was gonna tell us anyway!"

"I disagree, Doctor. I believe he was going to tell us to be careful!"

"That's kinda what I was driving at!"

The library doors dramatically burst inward like this is sone TV show, swinging theatrically on their hinges whilst a swirling, twirling breeze blows smoke and light into the room. It's showy and over the top and precedes the anticlimactic entrance of a four-foot high humanoid dressed in sneakers, blue slacks held up by braces - ask a grown-up! - a lime green t-shirt and black bow tie.

"That's…" Lieutenant Z'Dar starts saying, looking at the cover of his comic book until the being introduces itself.

"I'm Beezneez!"

"From the comic!" Z'Dar blurts.

"I am," Commander Mocha says, "Commander Mocha. First Officer of the Sol Ship Excel. We come in peace."

"Rather a silly name, don't you think!?" Beezneez says.

The Doctor laughs, "It's not wrong!"

"That's not…" Mocha says pointlessly, "…my actual name. My name is Ariana Mocha. I am Commander aboard the Sol Ship Excel!"

"Whatever you say!" Beezneez tries to approximate a shrug…badly.

"And Beezneez isn't a silly name!?" Mocha snaps.

The Doctor mutters, "Great diplomacy there, Commander!"

"Are you the one who created all this?" Lieutenant Z'Dar asks sensibly.

"All of what?" Beezneez asks.

"This." Commander Mocha replies, taking charge once more, sweeping her hand in a gesture that encompasses the buildings around them.

"I thought you did it!" Beezneez replies, trying to shrug once again.

"Beezneez." Commander Mocha says. "That is the name of a character in a comic book we found back there, which infers a direct connection to yourself, hence it stands to reason that you probably have some influence over our surroundings. Also, your life signs fluctuate in and of existence, or not at all, much like these very surroundings. These buildings have no substantiative value upon our equipment. If we did not see them, as we do now with our very own eyes, then they would not exist. It stands to reason, then, that you and our environment are linked somehow."

"Geez," Beezneez says, "you don't half waffle on!"

The Doctor laughs. "I agree. But the Commander does make a good point. What are you, and why are you here?"

"Why are you here?" Beezneez asks.

"We are explorers." Commander Mocha replies.

"I'm an explorer, too!"

"Where are you from?" Asks Doctor D. "What species are you?"

"I'm from here." Beezneez replies. "Where are you from?"

"We're from Earth." Doctor D replies with rising exasperation. "The Commander and I are humans, Lieutenant Z'Dar isn't, he's from a planet called Plannette."

"I'm not human." Beezneez says. "I'm not..."

"This isn't getting us anywhere!" Commander Mocha says with unhindered exasperation. "You are not real! These buildings are not real! We are returning to our ship."

Beezneez laughs as best it can. "I cannot permit that to happen. Sorry."

An energy burst emanates from the ring of light surrounding Beezneez, engulfing the trio from the Sol Ship Excel who momentarily writhe with mild discomfort.

"Not real, huh!" Doctor Kelly D says to Mocha. "Right now, it feels pretty real to me!"

On the bridge of the Excel, Triandos, who has reformed into a humanoid shape, concludes a potted history of its predicament.

"With your help, Captain." Triandos says.

"Is there any way we can...recharge your power here?" Asks Chief Engineer Scobryne.

"I don't think so." Triandos offers. "I can only do that on...Uraskus Prime."

"Which your criminal prisoner forced you to leave?" Captain Cirroc asks, for clarification after all the exposition we missed!

"That is correct."

"And my crew are on Uraskus Prime with this dangerous criminal." Captain Cirroc states. "Suggestions."

"I think we should help." Scobryne says. "Triandos's energy signature is severely depleted from when we first detected it coming at us from Uraskus Prime, Captain."

"I...might...die." Triandos states.

"Er...Captain." Lieutenant Commander Jones, from the helm, raises a tentative hand. "What if Triandos is...actually the criminal? What if...it was ejected from the planet by, you know, the good guy?"

"Why wouldn't I just take over this vessel?" Triandos suggests testily.

Jones shrugs, "I don't know, why don't you?"

"Are you suggesting I should do just that?" Triandos asks.

"With all your power..." Chief Engineer Scobryne lets her sentence hang in the air.

"My power is fading." Triandos says. "You said so yourself not a moment ago."

"You might be faking it."

"I wish I was." Triandos appears to sigh.

An alert beep-beep-beep emanates from the Chief Engineers console. She has been monitoring the signals from the landing party. The officer at the console next to her nods, swipes his touch-screen, and the view on the big front viewing screen zooms in on the planets surface. There is just one life-sign, displayed with a pulsating blue dot amidst an area of yellow.

"Captain!" The Chief Engineer urgently says with urgency. "We have lost the communication signal and life-signs of the landing party! I'm reading just one large energy signature," she points at the viewing screen for emphasis, "right there. It's coming from the vicinity of the landing party's last known position."

"Rhionas!" Triandos's voice is barely audible, its brightness fading in and out.

"What just happened?" The Captain demands.

"Didn't I just explain!?" Says an exasperated Chief Engineer. "And if I knew more, don't you think I would've said!?"

"We're all going to die!" Whimpers Jones.

"Eventually, Lieutenant Commander Jones!" The Captain says, adding heroically, "but not today." He points to an Ensign, seated at a console. "Ready a shuttle, Ensign. We're going to Uraskus Prime to find out what the heck is going on!"

"Oh- yes, sir." The female Ensign practically purrs at the thought of helping her Captain.

"You're with me, Ensign!" The Captain says.

"I sure am!"

"Scobryne! You have the bridge!"

"Oh. Er…thanks!?" Scobryne acknowledges.

"Come with us if you want to live," Captain Cirroc tells Triandos. The Captain, Triandos and the unnamed Ensign enter the elevator or lift. "Deck five!"

"Yes, Captain." Responds HEAL - that's the computer, just in case you've already forgotten!

The elevator or lift ascends.

"Er- Captain?" The Ensign says. "Aren't we supposed to be going to the shuttle bay?"

"Yes, Ensign."

"But…the shuttle bay isn't on deck five, sir!"

"Well spotted, Ensign. I was just testing you! Computer: deck seven, if you will."

The computer responds with an affirmative and they travel in silence to deck seven - the shuttle bay where Shuttle Thirteen has been made ready for them.

"Shuttle Thirteen, sir. I hope you don't mind?" Says the Ensign with slight trepidation.

"Ensign! What have I told you about researching ancient, archaic beliefs which grew out of favour on Earth hundreds of years ago? Scientists have proven irrefutably that the number thirteen has no bearing on one's luck."

"Aye, aye, Captain."

The two humans and Triandos board the shuttle craft.

"You have the helm, Ensign." The Captain declares.

"But…sir…I've not been trained as a pilot." The Ensign responds.

"Ah- well done, Ensign. That was another test!"

"Oh, Captain, you're so wonderful!"

Captain Cirroc takes the seat at the helm of Shuttle Thirteen - not an unlucky number in their century! He powers them away from the mothership - no pre-flight checks required, this is the future - aiming the shuttle at Uraskus Prime.

"How do you regenerate your life force?" Cirroc asks the blob of energy which radiates from within the cabin, casting its ever-changing rainbow of colours into all corners, but seemingly more faint than earlier on the bridge.

"My home…" Triandos's voice is weak, "…Uraskus Prime, and I…are bonded…my life…is part of…it's life."

"That's fascinating." The Ensign says with obvious sincere fascination.

"I agree." Captain Cirroc says in agreement. "Does your prisoner, the criminal, use that same energy?"

"Yes." Triandos replies weakly.

They fly the remaining distance to the surface of Uraskus Prime without incident, landing in the same barren wilderness next to the first Sol Ship Excel shuttlecraft. Triandos instantly vanishes in a burst of light. Captain Cirroc uses the shuttles scanners to locate any signs of life on the planets surface.

"That's odd." Says Cirroc to himself.

"What's odd, sir?" The Ensign asks, sidling close up to her Captain in the small cockpit, her big eyes widening as she looks at him.

"I'm picking up two energy signatures, but no lifeforms."

"The landing party?" The Ensign queries with concern, dramatically gripping the Captain's arm.

"Nothing."

"I wonder what's happened to them."

"I don't know. Hopefully they're safe. Maybe some…thing…or someone is blocking their life sign readings from our equipment."

The Ensign follows Captain Cirroc out of the shuttlecraft and into the barren wasteland, with the disparate sight of Waveney Close in front of them like a wraith shimmering in the heat, or like an oasis in the desert, or some other similar thing.

"Do you mind, Captain?" The Ensign asks as she holds his hand in hers. "I'll feel much safer."

"Not at all, Ensign."

The pair enter the outskirts of the village, it's road being remarkably incongruous by comparison to the otherwise desolate landscape. The Captain has his scanner in his free hand, the only energy source now registering upon it is further along Waveney Close. He touches an engineering application which is linked to his ship, and a biometric display shows him there is an abundance of the compound present, which was the cause of their stop-off at Uraskus Prime in the first place.

Captain Cirroc frees his hand from the warm grip of the Ensign, and taps his shoulder communicator: "Cirroc to Excel."

"Scobryne here, sir." Comes the immediate response.

"Just so you know, Chief Engineer, we have an abundance of that compound you require on the surface of this planet."

"That's good news, sir. If we don't get any, we won't be going much further."

The Ensign mutters: "Tell me about it!"

"Indeed, Chief Engineer. I'll keep you posted."

"Aye, aye, Captain."

Returning his hand to his side, the Ensign soon takes it in hers, shrugging gingerly.

"Don't worry, Ensign." The Captain says heroically. "I'll take care of you."

The Ensign mutters: "I wish you would!" She sighs with frustration.

They walk cautiously along the winding road, absorbing the tidy and organised atmosphere of the historically accurate village close-up. Each garden is neatly contained, each property different yet eerily similar. There are no signs of life whatsoever. The only sound is the footfalls of the Captain and the

Ensign - whose grip has tightened - and the monotonous beep-beep-beep of the hand-scanner, which directs them toward the source of energy.

Commander Mocha, Doctor Kelly D, and Lieutenant Z'Dar levitate one-foot off the library floor in a undulating light source. They are unharmed, can move within, but are incapable of affecting their escape or activating their communication devices and scanners.

Beezneez shimmers as if trapped within a bubble, it's rainbow colours constantly altering their appearance and shape. It follows the trapped trio toward the open door at the end of the library which contains the 'Bee Nee' comic books. The energy light source squeezes through the doorway, the people also safely passing through, hovering, until gently descending to the floor.

"The comic books..." Lieutenant Z'Dar says. "They must be the inspiration for this village and Beezneez appearance."

"That's a very astute observation, Lieutenant." Commander Mocha says patronisingly. "One which I had already made, but never mind! This Beezneez, or whatever the being is truly known as, has formed this village, this Waveney Close, on the presumption that we would be familiar with it based on its assumption the comic book would be a familiar one to an Earth ship. Clearly, this means Beezneez has the capability of scanning the Excel, and would also explain the appearance of a similar being, as the Captain described, onboard the Excel. The question is: is Beezneez being belligerent or protective? Is this energy life-form an antagonist or protagonist? And what is happening on the Excel?"

"That's a lot of supposition!" Doctor D says.

"Ha, ha, ha…" Beezneez laughs. "This is fun! I have decided I'm a protective protagonist! I like your language. Protective protagonist!"

"Do you know what either word means?" Doctor Kelly D asks, directing a look to Commander Mocha which indicates for her to be quiet - she sulks.

"Let me…" Beezneez says, "…what's the word in your language…think! Protective…yes. Protagonist…yes. Yes! Protective protagonist! I understand both words! And I am both."

"And the…being similar to yourself?" Doctor Kelly D prompts. "The one who is on our ship right now. How would you describe that one?"

Beezneez mimics a thoughtful pose before answering, "Angry antagonist! Ha, ha, ha… Angry antagonist! Angry antagonist!"

"Wow." Lieutenant Z'Dar says. "That comic book must be cool. You've mimicked some elements from it to become playful and childlike! I'm gonna take a few more copies back to the ship!"

"Help yourself." Says Beezneez.

"Er…that might be tricky!"

"Beezneez." Says Commander Mocha. "Might I ask how these…comic books…came to be here?"

"Yes." Beezneez replies.

After a brief pause, the Commander asks: "How did these comics come to be on this planet?"

"My planet!"

"Yes."

"Yes, what?"

"Yes. Your planet. How did these comic books come into your possession, so many light-years from Earth?"

"Good question…Commander."

Doctor Kelly D sighs, "In other words, you don't know!"

"I do, I do!" Beezneez replies excitedly. "A… vessel…like yours but not like yours! New but older! Came here! Crashed here!?"

"And they had comic books!?" The Commander says skeptically. "I wonder if they were hoping to colonise a planet and use these comics as a basis for inspiration."

"Sounds a bit stupid!" Doctor D scoffs.

"Sounds cool!" Lieutenant Z'Dar comments.

"My question," the Commander says, "was purely hypothetical."

Doctor D mutters: "More like simply pathetic!"

"What happened to the people onboard this vessel?" The Commander directs the question to Beezneez.

"What vessel?"

"The one which landed here, on your planet, with this collection of comic books?"

Beezneez approximates a shrug, laughs, shrugs again, laughs and does a little dance of shrugs around the room, under the bemused gaze of the trio of Sol Ship Excel crew members.

"They…" Beezneez says, "…were like you."

Doctor D mutters: "I hope not!"

"How many were there?" Commander Mocha asks.

"I don't know numbers."

"Well…let me see. There are three of us. Four, including yourself."

"Oh. There were more than four!"

"That's a start, at least. What happened to them?"

"Triandos!"

Doctor Kelly D asks, somewhat irritably, "What, or who, is a Triandos?"

"Triandos is Triandos." Beezneez replies. "Beezneez is Beezneez!"

"Triandos must be the other being," Commander Mocha concludes - maybe correctly, not to give the plot away! "The one on the ship. Captain Cirroc didn't say whether the being was malevolent or benign, but from what Beezneez says, this Triandos is responsible in some way for the disappearance of the comic book ship. And we haven't heard from the Excel in quite some time."

"But, Commander…" Doctor D begins. "Captain Cirroc clearly said…"

"…but we do not know if Beezneez can be trusted to tell us the truth." The Commander finishes. "Beezneez. In a show of faith, if you mean us no harm, can you release us from this energy field so we might try contacting our ship?"

"I can. But I'm not going to!"

Captain Cirroc and the disposable - whoops, my bad! - Ensign cautiously approach the open doorway to the library, stamping up the gravel pathway. They can see inside the building. It's a cavernous space which appears to be empty.

"Oh, Captain!" The Ensign presses her body against his. "I'm frightened."

"Don't worry, Ensign, I'll protect you." The Captain tells her heroically. "This building...this library...is really quite incongruous amongst this already incongruous village amidst the barren landscape. I wonder what it all means." He ponders.

They enter the library, their footfalls hollow, the lack of an echo in its emptiness unerring. Ahead of them is the staircase and doors, all of which are closed.

"Captain." Says the Ensign tremulously. "Shouldn't you get your weapon out as a precaution?" No innuendo here!

"What weapon?"

"The laser gun!" She sighs wantonly.

"Oh, yes. Probably a good idea! Besides, I've lost all readings on the scanner."

Captain Cirroc pockets the scanner and unclasps his hip holster, sliding out the laser gun - which is approximately the size and shape of a Walther PPK because everyone in the future is a James Bond fan!

"Pick a door!" The Captain says.

Still holding tightly onto her Captain's hand, the Ensign directs them towards the door furthest to the right. She grips the handle, turns it, and the door opens into a brightly lit empty room which has a double-door entrance to an elevator or lift shaft in the back wall. As they approach, the doors part. The elevator car is empty.

"I guess we go this way." Captain Cirroc says. "Throw caution to the wind, and all that!?"

They enter the empty car. The doors slide shut behind them. A panel beside the door interior indicates the levels: there are five to choose from, although they are all numbered four.

The Ensign takes her cue once again, pressing button number four - ? - and the elevator begins its imperceptible journey in whatever direction level four is, presumably downward, but their motion is negligible so it's impossible for the occupants to ascertain their exact location.

After sixty seconds of travel their movement ceases and the doors part. They are greeted by a dome-shaped robot in a bare anti-chamber.

"Excuse me!" The robot says indignantly in a robotic voice.

"Hello." The Captain says, and introduces himself and the Ensign. "We are from the Sol Ship Excel."

"What of it?"

"Who are you?"

"None of your business!"

"Can you tell us about Triandos and Rhionas?" Captain Cirroc asks patiently.

"I don't want to!"

"Why are you so grumpy?" The Ensign asks not unreasonably.

"Who are you calling grumpy?" The robot retorts and abruptly a beam of blue light courses across the room, striking the Ensign who is promptly enclosed within an energy sphere, rendering her immobile but not dead - at least, not yet!

"That wasn't very nice." The Captain admonishes. "We come here in peace and you attack us! If you didn't want us here why did you allow the elevator to bring us here?"

"I don't have a name! I'm just a metallic construct! The elevator is an illusion! You are still on the surface of the planet! Triandos and Rhionas are manipulating your actions! I was fashioned many of your Sol System years in the past from remnants of a ship which crashed here a hundred years ago. It came from Earth, like you. They formed me from it! They mean you no harm! But your kind cannot survive here! You need to leave or face destruction!"

"Okay. Thank you. That was a lot of information. But..."

The robot vanishes, as does the energy sphere which encases the Ensign, who falls into Captain Cirroc's arms - not unwillingly! Suddenly the lights go out but, when light returns, the barren wasteland gradually shimmers into existence around the duo. They are between the two Sol Ship Excel shuttlecraft and the village of Waveney Close.

"Oh, Captain! What just happened." The Ensign pleads, her face close to his, her innocent brown eyes filled with winsome tears.

"Everything is all right, Ensign. You're fine." Cirroc assures her, tapping his shoulder communicator. "Cirroc to Excel." He receives no response. "Blast, that's not good!"

The Ensign expels a sharp breath, "Captain!"

"What is it, Ensign?"

"Your rank, sir. But that's not the point right now! Look over there!"

She points towards a ridge of virgin blue mountains behind them. The lone figure of Doctor

Kelly D descends a crumbling, unstable slope towards them. She waves, smiling, when finally she has reached the bottom. Within moments the doctor is reunited with her colleagues.

"Oh, Captain," the Doctor pants breathlessly - yes, her too! "What's happening?"

"I was hoping you might be able to tell us, Doctor." The Captain replies.

"Well, I'm a Doctor...not..."

"Where are the others?" The Ensign asks.

Doctor Kelly D nods in the direction of the faux village, "They must still be with Beezneez."

"Who is...Beezneez?" The Ensign asks.

The Doctor tells them what has happened so far, the exposition, if you will, in a concise manner - at least more concisely than that which Commander Mocha would've attempted, much to everyone's relief.

"This energy being, Beezneez," the Captain says at length, "sounds much like the description of Rhionas, which Triandos gave us."

If the Doctor had any eyebrows she would raise them quizzically. "Triandos?"

The Captain goes on to explain his own exposition, also in a manner which one might consider to be concise, thankfully!

"Both these beings have separated us from the Excel." States the Captain obviously. "For what purpose, only they can say. It's not as if they require our technology or anything, they seem pretty powerful beings as they are." Understatement! "And if they gain their power from this planet, Uraskus Prime, then they can't be after our ship."

"Maybe they're just bored." Doctor Kelly D suggests.

"Perhaps, maybe."

"Maybe, yes."

"So…we're trapped here?" Asks the Ensign, tremulous once more, clinging to the Captain for comfort and support and just because she likes it!

"Yes, Ensign, we are." The Doctor says pessimistically.

"Way to go, Doctor!" The Captain says. "I'm fairly optimistic we shall escape from here, Ensign, otherwise how will we have more adventures exploring curious new environments, unless the remainder of our exploits are all to be told in flashback or on this planet?"

"What's flashback, Captain?" The Ensign asks innocently.

"It's an old storytelling term, Ensign, similar to exposition. Come on…let's find our shipmates."

The Captain leads them determinedly and heroically towards the village, the Ensign not letting go of his hand, just because, while the Doctor brings up the rear, so to speak.

The Doctor mutters lamely, "I'd rather find our shipmates on the ship!"

"What's your view on this Waveney Close village, Doctor." The Captain asks in a chirpy tone.

"About the same as yours, Captain. We're roughly the same height."

"Very funny."

"I was being serious!"

"And I meant why do think it's been created like this? It's a curious illusion to present, don't you agree?"

"Not really, Captain." Doctor Kelly D says with an exasperated sigh. "I thought I already explained it's perceived evolution, unless you need me to go into Commander Mocha's level of detail."

"Good grief no, Doctor! We would be off this planet before she finished."

The Ensign laughs, looking whimsically at her Captain give us strength!

"Who do think created this, Doctor?" Asks the Captain. "Triandos…the being who came onto our ship? Or Rhionas, posing as Beezneez?"

"They both seem as capable as each other, Captain." The Doctor says honestly.

"Like playful children." Says the Ensign offhandedly. "And what about the robot? He said he had been constructed from the ship which landed here with the comic books onboard."

"Doesn't anyone think it's weird," says the Doctor, "that a ship should be carrying literature of that nature? I mean, it's ridiculous."

"Remember Altrainian Four, Doctor?" The Captain says. "The creatures with the two…"

"Oh, yes! They were pretty ridiculous."

"I can't remember that." Offers the Ensign.

"I'll tell you about it sometime." The Doctor says, a twinkle of retrospection in her eyes - oh dear, not at all PC these days!

They reach the library, it's exterior unchanged but the doors are now closed and the Robot from earlier is outside like a vertically-challenged sentry.

"May we enter?" Captain Cirroc asks.

"Yes." The Robot replies.

"Okay..." the Captain says, anticipating a bit more resistance, but at this point the robot is fairly superfluous, so never mind.

The doors part for the three from the Excel. The library interior is unaltered, but the energy known as the being Beezneez is before them, hovering with an ethereal effect above the floor.

"Triandos?" Captain Cirroc asks.

"Beezneez." Corrects the Doctor.

"Rhionas." Adds the Captain.

"What the...?" Thankfully the Ensign doesn't get finished with her expletive.

Beezneez approximates laughter, "Beezneez is Rhionas! Rhionas is Beezneez! Triandos is neither!"

"Rhionas." The Captain says. "Where are my other crew members?"

"You mean...Commander Mocha and Lieutenant Z'Dar?"

"That's right."

For no particular reason, Beezneez/Rhionas does another interpretation of its shrug-dance routine from earlier, and whose to be judgmental.

"Triandos told us that you are a criminal!" The Captain shouts, which causes the being to stop its bizarre behaviour. "Is this true?"

"That's a lie!"

"Why did you set me free?" Doctor Kelly D asks. "And not the others."

"Free? None of you are free!"

"You mean," the Captain says, "we're trapped here?"

The Ensign takes a dramatic sharp intake of breath and practically wraps herself around Captain Cirroc, much to the Doctor's disapproval.

"No." Beezneez laughs. "I mean…you need to disable the force field which Triandos has used to render your equipment useless on our planet."

"But my hand-scanner is working." Captain Cirroc points out.

"It only appears to be working because Triandos wants you to believe it's working!"

"If Triandos is the criminal and you are not," says Doctor Kelly D reasonably, and a bit of exasperation, "why were our two shipmates not released with me?"

"But…they are released!"

The library walls shimmer around them before the building vanishes from existence, along with the village of Waveney Close itself. The crew of the Excel are now amongst the barren, mountainous wasteland, the true surface of this region of Uraskus Prime. The two shuttlecraft are directly behind them as if the crew haven't actually moved, while Beezneez remains like a spectral apparition before them. Forty yards away, now standing in the middle of nowhere, are a confused looking Commander Mocha and Lieutenant Z'Dar.

The Excel landing party's are reunited.

"It's good to see you both." The Captain offers.

"Captain." The Commander says. "I believe I have discovered the purpose of our being here."

"There's a purpose…!?" The Captain begins.

"…I know, Captain, the compound which our Chief Engineer requires!" The Commander interrupts with exasperation, but she can't help it, it's her nature. "That is our purpose. What I mean, is I believe I know why Beezneez manipulated us and our equipment in an attempt to prolong our stay, by offering us surroundings both alien and familiar, in the form of the village we were in moments ago. I also believe that Beezneez is the only being on this planet."

"Upon what are you basing this…"

"Hypothesis?"

"That's right."

"A few facts and the numerous discrepancies between the various sources of information that have been presented with."

"And this comic book." Lieutenant Z'Dar announces proudly, clutching the book in question.

Commander Mocha goes on to explain what has happened, using an extremely convoluted technobabble exposition where nobody gets a word in edge-wise, and everything is resolved and wrapped up in a neatly tied bow.

The End

Not really the end, though.

The energy being whose name we aren't really sure of - and probably don't care by now - imitates the whimpering it heard from the Ensign, who is clinging tightly to Captain Cirroc. "Beezneez is sorry!"

"Are you mocking me?" The Ensign asks furiously.

"Imitation is the sincerest form of flattery." Commander Mocha says, quoting an archaic term which nobody has used in three hundred years!

The Ensign suddenly, and unexpectedly, vanishes.

"What's going on?" Captain Cirroc demands.

Beezneez metamorphosis's into a closer approximation of a humanoid form. It is no longer a diaphanous form of light and energy. It is flesh and blood and hair and all the attributes one associates with the human form. The resemblance to the departed Ensign is uncanny. Gradually, clothing identical to the Sol Ship crew materialises across the human form - you filthy animal!

"Ensign?" The Captain asks hesitantly.

"Beezneez." Commander Mocha states. "As I surmised, Captain."

"I'm confused." Lieutenant Z'Dar says.

"You're confused." Doctor Kelly D mutters.

"What have you done to my Ensign?" Captain Cirroc asks Beezneez who resembles the Ensign but isn't the Ensign!

"Captain," says Commander Mocha. "If I might explain?"

"Do we have a..." The Captain tries to speak!

"This entity," Commander Mocha continues unhindered, "is the only being we have encountered since our arrival at Uraskus Prime. It is not an omnipotent being, its sphere of existence is this planet. And despite its evolved form it has the naïveté of an adolescent. It's recognition of humans is based upon the arrival of the first ship, the one which crashed here and contained the...comic books. It's interaction with the crew was brief, I believe, because the crew likely perished soon after their arrival. The comic book which Lieutenant Z'Dar so cherishes inspired this creature, this Beezneez, or Triandos or Rhionas."

"But how...?" Captain Cirroc says.

"...How did I reach this conclusion." Commander Mocha says. "By simple deduction, Captain. And observation."

Doctor Kelly D roles her eyes, "But how do we leave this planet, Commander?"

"By...asking nicely, of course!" The Commander says in a condescending, patronising tone which the crew of the Sol Ship Excel have become accustomed to - although that doesn't make it the right behaviour!

The Ensign looks as confused as the rest of us!

"Ensign...Beezneez." Says the Captain at length. "Please...can we return to our ship?"

The Ensign, Beezneez, Triandos or Rhionas looks from face to face, before saying: "Yes."

Abruptly or suddenly: "Lieutenant Commander Scobryne to landing party, do you read me!?"

"Yes we do, Chief." Captain Cirroc responds with undisguised relief. "We're on our way back, Chief."

"With the compound, I presume?"

"Oh yes, Chief. We wouldn't dream of returning without the MacGuffin Compound."

Later, on the bridge of the Sol Ship Excel, with many questions unanswered and exposition incomplete, things have returned to normal - twenty-fourth century normal, at least.

"Resume our course, Lieutenant Commander Jones." The Captain says to the officer at the helm.

"Are you sure, Captain?" Chiwetel asks with nervous trepidation.

"Of course." Captain Cirroc says, pointing a finger flamboyantly at the viewing screen. "Let's continue our planet hopping! So…what have we learned this time, Commander?" He asks cheerfully.

Doctor D mutters, "Absolutely nothing?"

"I believe that the moral of this story is: never judge a book by its cover!" Commander Mocha wisely states like she's the first person to have ever had this very idea.

Doctor Kelly D justifiably, and sarcastically, mutters: "No kidding, genius!"

"Also….being polite costs nothing." Offers Lieutenant Z'Dar naively.

Captain Cirroc nods agreement, "That's right, Lieutenant. It doesn't matter who or what we are dealing with, politeness costs nothing."

"Captain." Commander Mocha says. "Might I point out that you have both used an expression which has no significance in this century?" - nor any other! - "We do not use currency so the cost of things is meaningless, only one's moral duty to one's self."

"Thanks for that," the Captain says, "Commander Pedantic!"

"But what does it all mean?" Lieutenant Z'Dar asks innocently.

"On this occasion, Lieutenant," Commander Mocha says, "and I think the Captain would agree, there was no real meaning to be gathered from the energy being's behaviour. It was merely acting in a playful manner hoping to lure us into remaining longer on its planet than we had initially intended, but without putting us into danger through malicious actions. It certainly could've forced us if it had wished to, judging from the powers it possessed."

"Captain!" The helmsman, Jones, says. "What course shall I set, sir?"

"Well…" Captain Cirroc begins.

"Sorry to interrupt, Captain!" Commander Mocha says.

Doctor Kelly D mutters, "Hypocrite!"

"We are receiving a message from Admiral Picker at Earth Station Gamma."

"Splendiferous." Sighs the Captain. "On screen."

"No he isn't, Captain."

"Do we have to go through the same routine every time?"

"Sorry, Captain, but it seems so."

"Great! Can you please put Admiral Picker on the viewing screen?"

"That was one of the messages, Captain." Lieutenant Z'Dar offers innocently. "Politeness. And you said please."

"Indeed it was, Lieutenant. Thank you for noticing."

The viewing screen fades out from their forward image of the planet Uraskus Prime as they turn left, to be replaced by the stern face of Earth Station Gamma's commander, Admiral Nastroil Picker.

"Captain Cirroc." Picker's nasally drone bursts forth from the speakers.

"That's me!" Cirroc replies.

"What's the meaning of this?"

"Can you pick a more specific question, Admiral?"

"Why have you deviated from your assignment, Captain Cirroc?"

"My crew and I picked this course because we wanted to continue picking at the legacy of our forefathers, who were explorers. We cannot retreat at the slightest provocation. We cannot pick sides just because we are told to. We need to continue exploring the many regions of space, to discover previously undiscovered life forms. I picked this Sol Ship because of its capabilities to sustain a crew for an extended mission. Admiral Picker, we each pick our destiny, you picked yours by picking an Earth Station colony on the planet Gamma Major."

"Your rebellious actions are the equivalent of mutiny, Captain Cirroc!"

"I prefer…renegades, Admiral Picker. My crew and I are Space Renegades, if you will!"

There are multiple eye-rolls from his crew.

Admiral Picker stabs a finger at the viewing screen, "Look here, Captain! Your actions will not be tolerated!"

"I disagree, Admiral Picker." Commander Mocha interjects because she's been impatiently awaiting for the opportunity to do so. "With our data gathering capabilities and sustainable energy efficiency, we shall be lauded for our endeavours."

"You shall be chased around the galaxy like the rogues you are until you are all captured, Commander!" Bellows Admiral Picker.

"That sounds like splendiferous fun! Cirroc out."

The communication ends, and the view screen is filled with stars and space.

"You heard the man, Lieutenant Commander Jones!" Captain Cirroc says with a dash of the dramatic. "Put the pedal to the metal and hit the gas."

"Captain!" Commander Mocha says with an exasperated sigh. "Might I say that your use of obsolete twentieth century expressions is lost on the younger, less experienced crew members, who might not have reached so far back into Earth's historical archives to draw forth these, what are now, meaningless phrases."

Captain Cirroc nods, "Quite so, Commander Mocha, and thank you for endlessly pointing out my numerous faults, I don't know where I'd be without you."

"You are welcome, Captain."

Doctor Kelly D rolls her eyes and mutters: "Give me strength!"

SPACE RENEGADES

EPISODE TWO

(Original script July 11th 1985)

'TIME FOR TROUBLE'

Lieutenant Commander Chiwetel Jones's panicked tones emanate from the helm position on the bridge of the Sol Ship Excel: "Shield integrity breach is imminent, Captain!" A warning klaxon blares out to patently stress the potentially catastrophic situation.

"You make it sound more exciting than the reality of our potentially catastrophic situation, Lieutenant." Captain Xero Cirroc says calmly.

"Sorry, sir."

"No problem. Just manoeuvre us to starboard by ten point three degrees and we should be fine."

"Should be!?"

"Just do it, helmsman, before it is too late!" The Captain cooly steeples his fingers behind his head.

The Excel banks sharply starboard, causing some crew members not strapped in to lurch uncontrollably as the altering inertia destabilises the ship, and gravity momentarily fluctuates.

"Yeah! That was some G's!" The Captain whoops delightedly, much to the chagrin of the majority of his crew.

"Scobryne to the bridge." The voice of the Chief Engineer comes through the bridge speakers. "What's going on? We just experienced a massive power drain to the engines…not to mention the loss of gravity!"

"It's all splendiferous now, Chief." Says the Captain calmly. "We're just negotiating an asteroid field and came upon a real big one."

"Wouldn't it be a good idea to warn us ahead of time in the future?"

"That's a wonderful idea, Chief, and duly noted."

"Med-bay to the bridge!" Doctor Kelly D's voice replaces the Chief Engineers over the bridge speakers. "I have reports of injuries coming in from all over the ship. What's going on?"

"Sorry, Doctor, no time to explain if you need to attend to medical emergencies, so I shall debrief you later."

"Your cabin or mine?"

The warning klaxon ceases as abruptly as it began, and they are now presented with stars and open space on the viewing screen.

Lieutenant Commander Jones is sobbing with relief at the helm controls.

"Captain?" Commander Ariana Mocha says calmly from her station at the rear of the bridge, stroking her beard.

The Captain rolls his eyes, unseen by his first officer. His back had been turned during the entire episode and he has actually anticipated that she would be the first to complain, but had been wrong. Now he mentally braced himself for the onslaught.

"That's right." The Captain acknowledges.

"I'm detecting a small energy signature from what would appear to be a ship of unknown origin."

"Where?"

"Well…not on the bridge, Captain!"

"Nice sarcasm, Commander."

"Thank you, sir."

"But really, where is this other ship?"

"Approximately half a light-year straight ahead."

"Splendiferous. Lieutenant Jones. Slow us down."

"Aye, Captain." The helmsman acknowledges wearily.

"The ship appeared very suddenly, Captain." Commander Mocha explains. "Once we came out of that asteroid field I ran a full scan of the immediate vicinity but there was nothing to detect, absolutely nothing, then suddenly it was just there, and not like it flew in under a similar propulsion system to ours, it was almost as if it flickered into existence at the exact point it now occupies."

"That's very interesting, Commander. What could have caused this…anomaly?"

"I hypothesise the ship made a quantum jump, although I can detect no particles suggesting this procedure. Or maybe there has been some unique displacement within the space/time continuum which created a…corridor through space in which the ship was able to travel."

Lieutenant Commander Jones at the helm holds up his hand to offer his opinion: "Maybe our equipment is faulty, Captain."

Captain Cirroc nods thoughtfully. "Quite possible, Lieutenant…and you really don't need to hold up you hand every time when venturing a theory on the bridge."

"Aye, sir…I mean no, sir."

"Captain!" Commander Mocha says.

"That's right, Commander." The Captain replies, because it never gets annoying!

"I am now detecting fluctuations in the time fabric around the immediate vicinity of the ship." Commander Mocha says, her tone practically dripping with puzzlement. She strokes her beard thoughtfully once again. "It must possess a unique propulsion system, the likes of which we have not come across before. The space around it…folded temporarily, and I detected a momentary lapse of chronological synchronicity."

Lieutenant Commander Jones at the helm holds up his hand to offer his opinion: "Maybe our equipment is faulty, Captain."

"That was funny, Lieutenant." The Captain acknowledges.

"They've raised some kind of deflector shield!" Lieutenant Z'Dar at the tactical station informs everyone.

"I'm getting a sense of Deja vu." Says the Captain. "Lieutenant Z'Dar."

The younger, less experienced officer turns about in his seat, his big blue eyes looking loving at the Captain: "Yes, sir." His voice is silky, almost panting, in response to the Captain.

"Please raise our shields."

"Oh yes, sir, anything for you."

Their own protective deflector shields are raised like an invisible energy cocoon around the Sol Ship Excel, displayed upon the main viewing screen with a subtle green tinge before them. The other vessel is smaller than the Excel and looks incapable of causing any real threat to the Sol Ship.

"Alert status Alpha." The computer, HEAL, announces.

"They've lowered their shields, Captain." Lieutenant Z'Dar looks almost seductively at the Captain, because he's an irresistible alpha male!

"Thank you Lieutenant." The Captain grins.

At that moment there is a sparkling shaft of light on the bridge just in front of the viewing screen, and a male humanoid materialises out of apparently thin air. He is attired in bright but not garish colours.

"Hello, folk of the Excel!" The man says, his tone jovial and friendly but not ridiculously flamboyant. "My name is Bram Phil-Stone and I come from your future."

There are collective intakes of breath, coupled with groans of resignation from various members of the bridge crew, mainly because they can foresee that this revelation won't end well - and, I know, a time-travel story already!

"Of course you do!" Is the Captain's reticent response.

"Captain!" Commander Mocha says. "I did detect a minimal quantum shift upon this man's arrival."

"Look, I..." Bram begins, but we know the score by now!

"And its presence is consistent," continues Commander Mocha, "with the time fluctuations we detected when his ship blinked into our own scanner range."

"I..."

"There are residual particles on the bridge emanating from this man, but seemingly these pose no threat to us!"

Lieutenant Commander Jones sighs with resigned frustration, "Seems a bit easy for people to come and go as they see fit on this ship!"

"Commander Mocha!" The intruder pleads. "Captain Cirroc! Aren't you both at least a bit excited to have a visitor here from your future?"

Lieutenant Jones takes a sharp intake of shocked breath - better late than never.

"Sir!" Says Captain Cirroc, imperiously straightening his shirt like it's in some way significant to his alpha status. "How do you know who we are?"

Bram answers with a hint of perturbation, "I'm from your future!?"

Captain Cirroc nods thoughtfully, "I suppose there was a clue in that earlier declaration, but if we accepted everything on face value, sir, we would be dead long ago."

"True." Acknowledges Bram, looking around the bridge.

"It's a bit creepy, too." Comments Lieutenant Z'Dar.

"And who might you be?"

"I'm Lieutenant Z'Dar."

"Oh."

"What does 'oh' mean?"

"Where is the legendary Doctor Kelly D?" Asks Bram, hastily deflecting the question.

At her station, Commander Mocha's hairless brow furrows with puzzlement, "Captain! I've just intercepted an internal request for medical assistance for Doctor D to attend the engine room. It seems that not only has she failed to reach her destination, but all communication with her have been lost."

"Computer!" The Captain says into the ether, which doesn't look at all like he is in fact talking to himself. "Location of Doctor Kelly D, please."

HEAL responds in her electronic voice, "the Doctor is no longer aboard, Captain," like even the computer is flirting with our heroic, handsome Captain - weirdly awkward!

"Dude, where's my doctor?" Asks Captain Cirroc - an archaic reference which even Commander Mocha doesn't pick up on, mainly because it's sh….

"Umm- I expected her to be here!" Replies Bram innocently.

"Well she isn't!" The Captain states pointedly.

"Captain." Commander Mocha says. "According to the ships database, Doctor D disappeared an instant after our visitor arrived, which can be no mere coincidence, sir. It stands to reason both incidents are linked. I would hypothesise the quantum displacement of Bram's arrival has affected our reality."

Bram slaps his thigh, "Blast! How inconvenient! I was so looking forward to meeting the great Doctor, but just my luck, she's not here!"

"Didn't you hear what Commander Mocha just said?" Captain Cirroc asks with an accusatory tone. "The Doctor disappeared the same time you arrived!"

"Entirely inconsiderate, if you ask me!"

"And convenient."

"Inconvenient I would say, but...I had nothing to do with it."

"The penny drops! I want to know the person who did have something to do with it, huh...the tooth fairy?"

"Captain," say Commander Mocha, "may I point out your usage of yet another meaningless ancient Earth thing, this time the fairytale creation of the Tooth Fairy, which was..."

"Thank you, Commander!" The Captain sighs, before addressing Bram. "It isn't that I don't believe you, Bram, but having just met you...I don't believe you! Your appearance and the Doctor's disappearance are not merely coincidental. If you are from the future, our future, then it goes without saying that your technology is superior to our own, so threats would be wasted on you! So...please can we use our own plough-beam to bring your ship into our shuttle bay for examination?"

"As you asked so nicely..." Bram says.

"A moral from last weeks show!" Commander Mocha states with boredom.

"Lieutenant Z'Dar." The Captain says. "Lock on the plough-beam and bring Bram's ship aboard."

"Oh, yes, Captain!" Comes the sultry reply - he really can't help himself, the Captain is an enigmatic, virile, handsome guy.

"Computer...scan for all anomalous information regarding the disappearance of the Doctor." The Captain turns to Commander Mocha. "How about you and I escort Bram to the docking bay, Commander?"

"Aye, aye, Captain."

Doctor Kelly D's eyes flicker open and she is assailed by the tracking lights of an unfamiliar cubicle, although there are a pair of sliding doors in front of her, marking this out as possibly a lift or elevator. She realises she is moving: another clue? But this is no lift onboard the Sol Ship Excel.

She tries to think back to when she lost consciousness. She had been in a lift going from sickbay to the engineering section.

The lift stops, the doors part and...

"You are not...the Captain!"

"Ain't you the smartest!" Replies Doctor D.

Standing in front of the Doctor is a warrior from the oldest foe of the planet Earth, going as far back as when light-speed travel was first attempted at the end of the twenty-first century. These beings are collectively known as Trusk, owing to their nose protuberance in the form of a small trunk formed from a tusk-like hard shell. Their true name has always remained impossible for the translation devices designed by Earth scientists to decipher, despite all attempts and innovations. It is perhaps miraculous that the Trusk language has been translated, otherwise communication with them would also be impossible - not to mention slightly annoying for readers and writers!

"A...Doctor?" The Trusk asks, his two subordinates craning their necks to get a glimpse of the Earthling.

"Hey, correct again!" The Doctor says. "Who are you? Where am I? And why am I here?"

If a Trusk could display being unperturbed, then this one was doing the equivalent to that thing. "I am Adameve, ……. Commander. You are on my ship. And you are here because some foolish, soon to be deceased colleague of mine brought you to my ship instead of your Captain!"

"Yeah, okay…but how did you get me from my ship to yours?" The Doctor asks pointedly.

"We have come into the possession of a matter converter transportation device."

"A…what now?"

"Come with me…Doctor…and almost all shall be explained." The Trusk Commander instructs via the Doctor's translation device, because not everybody speaks English, even some English people have failed to master the language in this century, and centuries gone by!

Doctor Kelly D follows the Trusk called Adameve through unfamiliar corridors on this ship which is alien to her - you get the picture. The ceiling tracking lights do nothing to enhance the austerity of this vessel, at least in the Doctor's eyes, but she isn't aware of the Trusk's perception of colours and aesthetics, so cannot fairly judge.

The Doctor's sarcasm will probably go over this species head, but she cannot resist: "Interesting decor."

The Trusk officer bringing up the rear grunts in a way which could be perceived as either noncommittal or appreciation, it's impossible to tell for sure. Maybe he is the interior designer!?

When they reach the bridge of the Trusk ship, which so far as Doctor Kelly D can ascertain is situated somewhat illogically at the front of the ship - prime location to be shot at and hit first - a large half moon-shaped viewing window shows the Sol Ship Excel to be stationed, presumably unaware, in front of them. The asteroid field lays some distance behind the Excel, but it's swirling danger is clearly visible.

"Who are you?" A confused voice asks.

Doctor Kelly D examines the Trusk who has asked - a female, taller than the others, whose appearance and apparel seems more evolved than her counterparts. "You first!"

"My name is…Skyvyryk." The Trusk announces proudly, as if it should be significant which, in her future-time, it is!

"I'm Doctor Kelly D." The Doctor replies, nodding perfunctorily toward the Sol Ship Excel. "That's my ship. Where are you from?"

"Here."

"No you're not. My perception and your clothing says that you're not from this ship, despite being a Trusk."

"That is remarkably perceptive of you, Doctor. I'm from the future."

The Doctor shrugs like this sort of revelation occurs all the time. "What do you want with me?"

"Actually…nothing. We were after your Captain. But never mind, we shall make do with you."

"Charming! So you have a device to hide this ship from our sensors, that I understand, but what's that thing Adameve mentioned earlier…a matter transporter?"

The Trusk called Skyvyryk laughs with superiority: "It's from my time. I invented it." She lies proudly. "And my intention is to return balance to the force."

"Do what!?"

"In my time we have been cowed by an alliance with Earth and your allies. But I intend to bring this advanced future technology to our force in your time, so we might wipe out all possibilities of the Trusk being subjugated."

"And my Captain is presumably instrumental in this alliance occurring?" The Doctor ponders. "Which is a curious concept seeing that right now he and we are considered renegades by our our fleet."

The Trusk nods: "I agree, but in time you will be considered heroes of your Sol System."

"Is it not a bit reckless to give me details of the future?"

"No. Because the future, your future, will be altered here!" She laughs maniacally.

Captain Cirroc, Commander Mocha, and their visitor who claims to be from the future, Bram Phil-Stone, ride an elevator or lift - no, I'm not going to do that every time! - to the docking bay level.

"Bram," says the Commander at length, because she can't be edited concisely! "When you first came aboard the Excel, you appeared as if via some sub-space transportation system of a similar, if not identical, nature to how your ship first appeared. Are these devices somehow connected and, if so, how do they operate without causing physical particle or

DNA damage to the unit being brought through this procedure?"

Bram laughs, "I cannot tell you much, at least nothing technical. It's called a matter transporter. Scientists adapted the technology...oh, a hundred years ago!" He laughs. "Which would be about three hundred years into your own future. I forget where and when I am! The transporter was created by a race of beings which you are yet to encounter, and I won't say who, just in case that knowledge alters the timeline."

"Understood." Says Captain Cirroc. "Could...?"

"If you truly are familiar with the future," Commander Mocha says, stroking her beard, "then how come you didn't know about our Doctor's disappearance? It stands to reason that events have been recorded, and despite our status as renegades we are clearly no mere footnote, because otherwise you would not know where to locate us, or know our names. Also, even if your turning up here now has somehow already altered the future timeline, then these events would have been recorded as thus and this new timeline would be the one of record in our future."

"A paradox, Commander." Bram says thoughtfully. "And a mystery which we shall have to unravel together."

"One other thing..." Captain Cirroc begins.

"...you still have not explained your reason for being here." Commander Mocha finishes.

"That's not what I was going to say!" The Captain says. "I was wondering if this...matter transportation technology...might've been responsible or the disappearance of Doctor D?"

Bram claps his hands together delightedly - but not in a childish fashion! "Yes, yes, that's a possibility...which means I was correct...probably! I told my...that is your...that is Earth's...that is...!"

The elevator stops, it's doors part and they enter a corridor which leads into the docking bay. They walk and talk like multitasking is taken for granted in the future.

"I realise this is confusing," says the Captain. "And I understand your reluctance to give anything away about our future, even inadvertently, but if you can shed some light on these matters, even with conjecture, that would be appreciated."

Bram nods. "Yes, yes." He gathers his thoughts. "On an earth colony which has yet to be settled...I won't reveal when that occurs, for obvious reasons...we were visited by this culture which possessed the matter transportation system. I was born on that colony fifty years later, that is...well, many years into your future, but fifty years ago in my past. Anyway...unnecessary exposition later...a scientist on my colony discovered a way to manipulate this device to send somebody through time and, as with all great inventions, somebody wanted to use it as a weapon! It was stolen by...the race you know as Trusk. We still retain the prototype, which I subsequently used to follow a Trusk scientist to this specific point in time."

Commander Mocha strokes her beard thoughtfully and is about to dominate the conversation...

"We're still in conflict with the Trusk?" Asks Captain Cirroc like he's the one in charge, which he is!

"No, no, no…but like all races there are those dissidents who openly oppose the slightest notion of change." Bram patronisingly explains. "Blah, blah, blah! This Trusk, the one I'm after, is a leading scientist in their society, but moonlights as an evangelical rabble rouser extolling the virtues of Trusk halcyon days."

"Presumably the ship they are on," says Commander Mocha, "has stealth technology which renders it invisible from scanners and to the naked eye."

The doors into the docking bay automatically slide open. Amongst the four shuttlecraft - No.'s 1, 5, 7 and 13 - is Bram Phil-Stone's sleek, futuristic vessel. Technicians are busy doing technician things. They are met by Chief Engineer Mathilde Scobryne.

"Hi!" The engineer's greeting to her Captain accompanies a look of longing, while she gives the Commander a perfunctory nod, and Bram a look of disdain. "That your ship?"

Bram's eyes are bright, "Yes, yes, that's it. My name is Bram Phil-Stone," he extends a hand in greeting, "and you are the legendary Chief Engineer Mathilde Scobryne. It's an honour to meet you, I've read all your electronic manuals."

To Captain Cirroc, the engineer asks: "Who is this weirdo?"

"He's from the future." The Captain replies.

"That explains a lot."

Bram Phil-Stone explains the same exposition to the Chief Engineer which he has already said to the others, about his reasons for being here and how he got here, blah, blah, blah.

"That's actually interesting." Engineer Scobryne acknowledges, which causes the Captain to raise his eyebrow.

"May we look inside your vessel, Bram?" Captain Cirroc asks smoothly.

"Of course."

"Captain!" Commander Mocha interjects, which we have come to expect by now! "May I return to the bridge and carry out scans of this area of space for a cloaked ship? There is a very high probability that there is some form of spacial distortion or disturbance from a Trusk vessel which we might very well be able to detect."

"Yes, yes, of course." The Captain agrees without hesitation.

The Commander promptly departs by the same way in which they arrived, while Bram Phil-Stone leads Captain Cirroc and the Chief Engineer to his awaiting ship, a small, futuristic-looking craft which is more futuristic than the Sol Ship Excel - of course it is!

Bram touches a device on his utility belt which opens the entrance hatch to his ship, and he leads them both aboard - cautiously, of course, because these people aren't stupid, it might be a trap!

"If we found the cloaked ship," suggests Scobryne, "could we use your matter transportation device to get us across to them?"

"Sadly, no." Bram says. "It is calibrated solely to an individual's DNA signature. These are highly complicated devices which cannot be used with flippancy."

"And the time jump thing? Why don't we just use that to got back before this Trusk scientist got here so we can prevent whatever she intends doing?"

Bram laughs, slightly embarrassed: "If only it were that simple. The time jump is…one way."

"Figures." The Engineer says.

"Which means," says Captain Cirroc, "that neither you nor the scientist can return."

Bram nods without sadness because his goals are worthy of the cause he is set upon achieving.

"Nice ship." The Engineer offers her appraisal. "Lots of things have changed in your time, I guess."

"Technological innovations of humankind have always made progress." Bram laments. "Yet the evolution of our species itself has been slow. You are now considered as…renegades, which implies the powers that be, those who have placed themselves in charge on Earth, have yet to evolve beyond their own beliefs and ethical values. History…my history…was written by the victors and waters are slightly muddied, yet it seems that the human race has fundamentally improved." He nods thoughtfully. "But my ship, yes, it has lots of wonders which enable a lone pilot to crew it, but essentially the bare bones are the same."

"You sound like my first officer." Captain Cirroc mutters - mainly because the Doctor is elsewhere and she mutters…a…lot!

Speaking of whom…!

* * * * *

Doctor Kelly D is seated and strapped to a chair on the bridge of the Trusk spacecraft, with an admittedly lovely view of the Sol Ship Excel afar, but she isn't at her most comfortable.

The Trusk Commander, Adameve, is looming as menacingly as he can over her shoulder. He brandishes an object which resembles a syringe, only with a more futuristic and alien design - visually it keeps things simple and at a level of human understanding!

"I hope you don't mind if I implement a mind-scan on you?" Adameve asks quite convivially.

"I object!" Says Skyvyryk.

"Not on you," the Commander says, "the human!"

"I knew that!" Skyvyryk rolls her eyes, which is a pretty grotesque sight because their eyeballs protrude from their sockets!

"I object too!" Says Doctor Kelly D. "I heard those things can be lethal!"

"There is a possibility of brain damage, yes." Adameve states matter-of-factly.

Doctor D mutters: "And I wouldn't want to be like you guys!"

Skyvyryk throws her head back and laughs boisterously, which turns a few Trusk heads with curiosity because this race aren't renowned for their sense of humour - basically it's nonexistent!

"We have…evolved." Skyvyryk says by way of explanation to the curious. "And besides, there's no point torturing this particular human, she's of no use to us other than as a bargaining chip with her Captain."

Doctor D mutters: "Charming!"

"I suggest," Adameve barks at Skyvyryk, "you use your transportation device to get her Captain here immediately, otherwise this opportunity will be lost!"

Skyvyryk sighs, or at least the Trusk approximation of a sigh: "You fool, Adameve! It's not as simple as just making it so! I admit to my mistake the first time, but these devices are complex and I shall need to perform the next transport myself!" She says smoothly. "My…improved design to this device limits its usage because you do not have the appropriate energy requirements in your century. If it breaks, we cannot repair it. As it is…I cannot return back to the future to get more of what I require!"

Doctor Kelly D clears her throat. "Er, excuse me, but if you're from the future and your scheme right here and now succeeds, couldn't we logically conclude that this energy you require to power your transportation device might in fact be available sooner, because you know what it is? Also, and I don't like pointing out this obvious timeline possibility, but your device may very well be more readily available in your time, too, if you have succeeded right now! Thus…you should be able to travel back to your century…like, you know, right now!"

Adameve stares hard at Skyvyryk, he too realising the sound temporal logic which the Doctor is espousing.

Skyvyryk stamps a foot, like she is an impetuous child or an adult who should know better! "I suppose there's only one way of finding out!" She presses the appropriate button on the time-jump device but nothing happens. "There!"

"So...we fail!?" Adameve asks reasonably.

"Not necessarily." Skyvyryk retorts. "I might have inadvertently created an alternative timeline when travelling here."

Doctor Kelly D snorts her derision. "That's a bit convenient, not to mention convoluted!"

"One error too many already!" Adameve states.

"I want this to succeed as much as anyone," Skyvyryk says scoldingly, "otherwise why would I come to this timeline with no way to return? Let me make my calculations," she taps at her transportation device.

"My patience wears thin!"

Doctor Kelly D mutters: "Your patience!"

"There!" Skyvyryk announces. "Now stand aside, my ungrateful comrade, I shall return with the Captain shorty." She activates her device and promptly a dazzling, shimmering light show ensues - cool!

In Bram's spacecraft aboard the Sol Ship Excel, Chief Engineer Mathilde Scobryne is gliding her hands above the flat-screen helm controls of the small vessel, watched by a nervous Captain Cirroc and calm Bram Phil-Stone.

"What does this button do?" Scobryne asks like an irritating child who won't leave things alone.

"Please don't!" Bram protests. "Your clumsiness is recorded along with your genius."

"My genius!?" Scobryne asks.

"And clumsiness!" The Captain reminds her. "When you performed your…time jump, Bram, we recorded a quantum field disturbance. Isn't it possible the Trusk had the same issue? We might not have witnessed it because of our entanglement with the asteroid field, but might your ship have recorded such a disturbance?"

"And the transportation of Doctor Kelly D?" Suggests the Chief Engineer. "Come to think of it… the Trusk scientist must've improved your design somehow. Like you said…it's DNA encoded for you only and cannot be altered." She beams. "I am a genius!"

"Well done, Chief." The Captain congratulates her. "Well, Bram?"

Bram nods acknowledgment and activates one of the flat-screen panels, swiping and tapping a few commands. The screen changes its configuration, showing a variety of futuristic - I know! - multi-dimensional graphics with words and figures extrapolated from a few thousand computational models, until finally it settles upon a single image.

"Voila!" Bram announces with satisfaction.

"What's that mean?" The Chief Engineer asks.

"I know!" Says the Captain excitedly. "Voila is an old Earth word which roughly translates as success!"

Bram indicates a flashing yellow dot amidst the detailed image upon the screen, "That's my ships signature when I arrived," he explains, before pointing at a white dot, "that's your ship, Captain." Finally, he indicates a green dot, set approximately between the two, "and that is the Trusk."

"Voila, indeed!" Comments Engineer Scobryne.

"Commander Mocha to Captain Cirroc." The voice of the Excel's first Officer emits from the ether.

"Cirroc here."

"Captain. I have been able to locate a cloaked Trusk ship at ten point three miles off our port bow." The Commander announces. "I was able to do this by…blah blah blah…" She doesn't actually say blah blah blah, but the technobabble she spouts isn't that interesting so we can skip to the conclusion. "…and I triangulated it using the asteroid field as a beacon."

Captain Cirroc yawns, "Well done, Commander." Then he mutters to Bram and Mathilde. "Could've cut the description in half!" Then, aloud: "Our guest has also located the Trusk vessel, Commander. He is going to attempt to use his…transportation device to go over there shortly."

"Understood, Captain…although as I am taller than yourself and most people aboard the Excel, I would appreciate not being called shortly!"

Everyone is a very bad comedian in this century, and all previous centuries, perhaps, but who am I to judge?

The Captain laughs feebly, pityingly. "Thanks Commander. Cirroc out. So, Bram, I suppose it's worth a try, but be careful. Whenever you're ready, I guess."

Bram nods. He activates his transportation device in a dramatic flourish, and a shimmering light show ensues - cool! - but after an anticlimactic split-second, Bram Phil-Stone reappears!

Or does he…?

Onboard the Trusk spacecraft, Skyvyryk is standing on the bridge in exactly the same place where she has activated her own transportation device. Doctor Kelly D watches with perplexed curiosity while the Trusk commander, Adameve, is outright hostile with annoyance.

"What…just…happened?" The commander demands. "Why did you not leave and where is her Captain?"

Skyvyryk stares blankly at Adameve. She looks around the bridge of the ship, at the faces, at her reflection in one of the computer screens, with abject confusion.

"I don't know!" Skyvyryk replies hesitantly, absorbing her surroundings - we know what's going on though, don't we?

Doctor Kelly D asks: "You need a doctor? You don't look well! Maybe that transportation thing isn't all it's cracked up to be?"

Skyvyryk studies the Doctor with recognition, not as if she were still Skyvyryk, but as Bram the time-travelling human from the future - shock, horror, revelation! Bram looks down at his hands which are not his own, a stupid act because he knows that to reveal what has happened would likely be a fatal error of judgement.

"I…must…" Skyvyryk says falteringly, his voice not his own, "…check the device." Calmly, he methodically unclasps the unit from his utility belt, focusing his mind on the problem at hand, ignoring the faces looking at him expectantly. What must they think of him? An imposter in a Trusk body? He must not draw any unnecessary attention to himself! Herself!? He must not panic! Bram wonders if the same thing has occurred to the Trusk scientist, the woman, and how she is coping with roles reversed.

"Explain yourself!" Commander Adameve demands. "Before you regret my impatience!"

Explain myself!? That might tricky! "It seems as though…" Skyvyryk stumbles over her words, "…I miscalculated. Maybe…maybe the time jump affected this unit. The…the device is still working, of that I am positive. I just need to make a few calibrations."

"Make them quick!"

The device in Bram/Skyvyryk's hands is practically identical to the one he is accustomed to, with slight modifications that appear cosmetic, but cannot be purely so. His own device wouldn't allow cross DNA usage, which implies the Trusk scientist, his quarry, has improved upon the original device. Bram tries not to panic, or raise his hopes.

"Can I go now?" Asks Doctor Kelly D. "Although I don't favour having my atoms torn apart by that futuristic device. Maybe I can borrow a shutter? I mean…you don't need me now really, do you? Plus I'm getting hungry and, oh boy, you don't want to make me hungry!"

"We are hungry, too?!" Adameve says. Wet eyes bulging hungrily, he takes the Doctor's chin in his hand. "You would make a fine meal."

"That's not exactly what I had in mind."

"Then I suggest you be quiet."

The Doctor mutters. "I shall try, but it's not easy."

"Skyvyryk!" Adameve bellows! "What's taking so long? We are running out of time! Despite these humans being stupid barbarians they are bound to lock onto our position at some point! My patience is limited, so I suggest you hurry it up!"

Skyvyryk/Bram pretends to study the device in his hand, but his mind is trying to conjure a plan. "Your cloaking system!" She says. "That can be the only explanation." And a way I can escape from here! "In my time our devices are much more sophisticated and permit this technology, our transportation devices, to work efficiently. They allow…these to function! Show me your operating system. I might be able to reconfigure it, despite this ships primitive nature."

Adameve is hesitant at first but eventually relents. "You!" He barks at one of his bridge officers. "Set up that console as our esteemed visitor requests! " Then, with no need to veil the implied threat, he says to Skyvyryk: "This had better work."

"Captain!" The voice of Lieutenant Commander Chiwetel Jones, presently at the ships helm and operational controls, bursts forth with panic from the Captain's personal shoulder communicator.

"Cirroc here." The Captain responds automatically, while his eyes and mind regard the confused contortions of expressions on the face of Bram Phil-Stone who, a mere second ago, had activated his transportation device but seemed to shimmer from existence without actually departing.

Chief Engineer Scobryne activates her personal scanning unit, which might as well be a system augmented to her own, because she is barely without one in hand.

"Ships long-range sensors have detected a Sol Ship fast approaching, Captain!" Announces the Lieutenants panicked, quavering voice. "That can't be good, can it!?"

"Calm down, Jones." The Captain heroically responds. "Commander Mocha, can you give me more details," he says into the ether then regrets the usage of the word 'details!'

"As you wish, Captain," Commander Mocha's reply is almost gleeful. "Five seconds before Lieutenant Commander Jones set off the alarm, Captain, our own inertia and that of the shifting asteroid field permitted our scanners to reach back whence we came, and they immediately detected the location beacon of the Sol Ship Bucktoo, presumably en route from its Earth Colony base, to our present position with, also presumably yet its probably current to assume, the aim of reclaiming our renegade vessel and crew."

"And…breathe!" The Captain laughs. "Okay. How long before it reaches our position?"

"Five minutes, thirty-three seconds, Captain."

"Captain." Engineer Scobryne's prompting voice is calm, and despite the dire situation, she cannot help but also sound seductive when addressing her supremely attractive superior officer.

Captain Cirroc looks first at the Engineer's perplexed expression as she studies the readouts upon her hand-held scanner, then at Bram Phil-Stone, who is standing rigidly in place with very evident consternation writ large. The human from the future grinds his jaw, eyes large and searching, while he stressfully clenches and unclenches his fists.

"What's happened?" The Captain asks.

The body-swapped Bram/Trusk scientist throws up his/her hands with confusion, "I don't know." He/she manages to utter.

"I was detecting an extreme fluctuation of unusual neutron radiation from our visitor, Captain." The Engineer announces. "Which have now dissipated on a subatomic level. Also, his matter transportation device seems depleted of the energy reading which I was detecting earlier on."

"Bram?" Captain Cirroc prompts the time traveller out of his reverie. "Any suggestions?"

Bram/Skyvyryk stares blankly back, opening and closing his/her mouth like a fish, before: "I'm…confused…Captain Cirroc. But…I must return to…"

"Captain!" The urgent voice of Commander Mocha bellows urgently from the communications system and, in the same instance, the Sol Ship Excel's alert klaxon starts blaring with equal urgency. "A Trusk vessel has lowered its cloaking technology. Their weapons are powered up!"

"Are they…" The Captain starts saying.

"Captain!" Mocha again. "Doctor D just appeared on the bridge with a Trusk!"

"Helmsman!" Captain Cirroc shouts. "Full speed ahead!"

A boom and shudder rocks the vessel, knocking Bram/Skyvyryk off his/her feet, but the two Excel officers stand their ground like seasoned sailors.

"Captain!" Commander Mocha again. "The Trusk vessel fired at us as we applied power to the engines, but we are safely away."

The Captain is visibly relieved. "That's a relief. Well done, everyone. Chief Engineer, get to the engine room. Make sure nothing is damaged."

"Aye, Captain." She responds and departs hurriedly.

Bram/Skyvyryk shakes his/her head, prone on the floor with dazed confusion.

"Captain!" The voice of Doctor Kelly D is filled with urgency as it comes over the intercom.

"Welcome back, Doctor." The Captain says suavely.

"Thank you, sir." The Doctor responds in a less that appropriate tone, considering the situation! "I… Captain…that is…the person you have with you…"

"Bram." The voice of Commander Mocha says.

"Bram isn't really Bram." The Doctor announces somewhat cryptically, causing Captain Cirroc to regard the shaken human clambering unsteadily to his feet, suspiciously. The Doctor continues: "If you come to the bridge, sir, all will be revealed."

The doors to the docking bay open and two burly security guards enter, striding with focused authority to the time travellers ship.

"Commander Mocha ordered us here, sir." One of them responds to the Captain's unspoken question.

"Understood." Captain Cirroc responds, and looks Bram in the eyes as the time traveller gathers his wits and stands. "If you don't mind accompanying us, Bram." He indicates with his hand toward the door and awaiting security guards.

Anger crosses Bram/Skyvyryk's face, but it's slightly contorted because the Trusk scientist is in an unfamiliar body. Her mouth moves but she cannot articulate the words. Finally, without protestation, the Trusk in human form does as Captain Cirroc instructs and the quartet make their way hastily to the bridge, where the Trusk who is now Bram, and Doctor Kelly D, are awaiting them, along with the regular bridge crew.

"I'm scared, Captain!" Lieutenant Jones announces from the helm controls.

Doctor Kelly D mutters: "Nothing new there!"

"Everything will be fine, Lieutenant Jones." Says the Captain with a confident smile. "Anyone care to explain what's going on because, quite frankly, I'm lost."

Commander Mocha clears her throat and strokes her beard, which means we're going to be here for quite some time: "Captain, If I might offer my detailed theory based on the numerous facts which have thus far presented themselves."

Doctor Kelly D sighs.

Captain Cirroc opens his mouth.

Neither get the opportunity to say anything, because Commander Mocha is on a roll: "It would seem that our time travelling duo have unexpectedly and inexplicably swapped bodies."

The silence draws on because everyone was expecting a long and intensely detailed account of the situation from the usually long-winded Commander, but no, that's it!

"Okay. Thank you, Commander." Says the Captain, perplexed. "Is there any way of reversing the situation?"

"I hope so!" Bram in the Trusk body says indignantly.

Skyvyryk in Bram's body gesticulates as best she can, making guttural sounds which don't translate, cowed by the two security guards which stand either side of him/her.

"And," the Captain says to Commander Mocha, "what of the Trusk vessel? Are they pursuing?"

"Yes, Captain." The first officer replies.

"We're doomed!" Simpers Lieutenant Jones.

"With the Sol Ship Bucktoo following the Trusk ship." Commander Mocha adds.

Captain Cirroc nods thoughtfully, assessing the situation like the Captain he is!

"What about us!?" Suddenly and abruptly the Trusk in Bram's body has found her/his voice, pleading loudly. The futuristic transportation controller is in her/his hands but she/he stares at it with futility - there is no power to it.

Bram in Skyvyryk's body holds up his/her hands: "I cannot live like this!" He/she too has the similar transportation device in his/her hand but, again, it also shows no signs of power.

"Suggestions, anyone?" Captain Cirroc asks, hiding his abject embarrassment that he has absolutely no suggestions whatsoever.

Lieutenant Jones holds up his hand: "I have none, sir."

"Thanks for your honesty, Lieutenant." The Captain acknowledges, gratefully and guiltily.

"I suggest Doctor D take our guests to medical, Captain." Commander Mocha says calmly. "There she will be able to properly assess their situation. While that is taking place, we can monitor our pursuer - pursuers - and decide on the appropriate actionable steps for our own safety."

Captain Cirroc acknowledges these suggestions with a nod. "I concur. Doctor D, with our guests permission, of course."

"Aye, Captain." Doctor Kelly D responds, beckoning to the body-swapped time travellers, both of whom nod subserviently…they really have no options left to them, resistance futile - sorry, couldn't resist, so to speak! The doctor leads them to the lift and, before they are gone…

"Presumably Bram's ship cannot traverse time once more!?" Asks Commander Mocha.

Captain Cirroc shakes his head, and an idea pops in there! "It was a one-way journey. But…" He calls across to the departing trio: "Whichever one of you is the Trusk scientist! Can your ship be used for time travel any more?"

Bram/Skyvyryk shakes his/her head - a universal gesture for 'no' - just as the elevator doors close.

"What are we going to do, Captain?" Lieutenant Jones blubbers from the helm.

"Might I make a suggestion, Captain?" Commander Mocha ventures.

"Not yet, Commander." The Captain replies. "I'm thinking."

Captain Cirroc walks slowly around the bridge of the Sol Ship Excel, stopping at each manned station: he offers Lieutenant Jones a reassuring pat on the shoulder when the helmsman shows him their flight readouts. Next, the Captain stops at the tactical station, where Lieutenant Z'Dar shows his Captain relevant system reports pertaining to their present situation - the Lieutenant sighs wanly at the Captain's manly confidence. Finally, Captain Cirroc studies readings on Commander Mocha's display, which shows the flight trajectories of all three ships, beginning with the Excel, and various projected scenarios.

Captain Cirroc nods thoughtfully: "Is there any chance the Trusk vessel will intercept us before the Bucktoo reaches them, Commander?"

"Unlikely, Captain." The Commander replies.

"That's jolly splendiferous then!" The Captain claps his hands together, satisfied the situation isn't as dire as it appeared moments previously. "All we need to do is evade the Trusk ship, the Bucktoo, and see if we cannot somehow figure out a way to separate our time travelling duo."

Commander Mocha clears her throat, preparing herself to launch into... "Unless our doctor can perform miracles, Captain, I cannot see any way whatsoever that our current technology can be utilised to perform an act which, purely by accident, was created by the time travellers' futuristic hardware which, owing to circumstances after their arrival which we are aware of, the technology has subsequently been rendered obsolete, namely, destroyed, which we would not have been able to replicate anyway. Our best option is to prepare the time travellers for the inevitability that they will be spending the remainder of their lives in the others body, however unappealing that prospect might seem to both parties, it's something they will have to accept….not to mention that they are both guilty of causing this body-swapping by their antics, one who wanted to alter their timeline, the other for following to prevent something which might not actually have occurred anyway. Paradoxically, and to use an archaic Earth term, which I'm sure you will appreciate, Captain, but it would seem they have reaped what they have sown."

Captain Cirroc waits for more from the Commander who, when in full flow, can talk for hours! But, eventually, and after a moments silence, he nods slowly in acknowledgement. "Lieutenant Jones." He says to the helmsman. "Plot a course which allows us to evade detection from the Trusk ship and the Bucktoo."

"Captain!" Says Lieutenant Z'Dar. "If the Bucktoo engage the Trusk ship in combat shouldn't we offer assistance?"

"The Trusk are no match for the Bucktoo, Lieutenant. Don't worry. I wouldn't just abandon our own people if I believed there was any threat to them, despite their obvious aim to capture us."

"Aye, Captain."

Lieutenant Jones says, his voice more calm than it was earlier, "Course plotted, sir."

"Thank you, Lieutenant. Initiate at your leisure." Captain Cirroc smiles, looks around his bridge, satisfied that everything is under control. "Commander Mocha, you have the bridge."

In the ship's infirmary, Doctor Kelly D has both Bram and Skyvyryk on adjacent examination tables,. They are hooked up to various medical equipment to monitor their vital signs - basically futuristic tech which is beyond this authors comprehension!

Doctor D is studiously examining a handheld touchpad device when Captain Cirroc arrives. She looks at him and swoons. He looks at the two time travelling visitors, sedated - them, not he!

"Was it necessary to put them to sleep, Doctor?" The Captain asks.

"That depends upon your definition of necessary, Captain! They needed…calming down…so that's what I did!"

"Fair enough. I trust your professionalism, Doctor. Where do we go from here?"

"My cabin."

'I mean regarding their predicament."

Doctor D smiles, "There's nothing I can do for them, Captain…but I can do something for you!"

"Hmmm…that'll be wonderful…but will have to wait, I'm sorry to say. Commander Mocha did explain at great length before I came here that she was extremely doubtful we could offer any solution to this predicament."

"Yeah. These two are gonna have real fun adapting to their switcharoo!"

"We need to locate a facility which is equipped to handle them better than we can."

"You mean...dump the problem on someone else?"

"Basically."

"Sounds good to me. I don't think I could handle the inevitable psychological consequences their body swap will have on them both!"

Captain Cirroc laughs: "What sort of Doctor are you?"

"I'm not a psychologist...although I don't mind analysing you, sir!"

The Captain nods absently, as if he hadn't heard yet another of her suggestive comments which one wouldn't exactly describe as subtle.

"Couldn't we just load them onto Bram Phil-Stone's ship and, you know, encourage them to leave?" The Doctor suggests.

"That's a very ethical suggestion, Doctor!" The Captain replies facetiously, before contemplating the notion. "Although...it might be an option."

"I wasn't being entirely serious."

"I realise that, Doctor, and yet...it's worth making the suggestion to them." He indicates the two prone and unconscious time travellers with a somber nod of his head. "Obviously we cannot merely dispose of them like some unwanted flotsam. It's a hard one."

The Doctor is about to comment.

"Decision, that is." The Captain says hastily. "Commander Mocha!" He says into the ether, getting an instant reply. "Report to the infirmary, please."

"Aye, Captain." The reply comes.

"Can you wake them, Doctor?" The Captain asks. "Gently, though. They've already had enough shocks…and there's another big one on the way."

The Doctor mutters: "Promises, promises." She cautiously carries out the Captain's request of bringing her patients around, monitoring their condition - because the future isn't magic! - just in case something goes wrong, because it's better to be safe than sorry, always has been, always will be!

Bram Phil-Stone and the Trusk, Skyvyryk, exchange glances, remaining on their respective examination tables, looking from the other to themselves, their new selves, both attempting to become attuned to this confusing situation which they are in.

Commander Mocha arrives from the bridge.

"Any news on the two ships?" The Captain asks.

"There has been no significant change, Captain." The Commander informs him. "Although according to our long range sensors the Trusk vessel appears to be altering its course very slightly. Whether that is to evade the Bucktoo, which they correctly perceive as a superior threat, or to counter our own course, is impossible to confirm at this time."

"Thank you, Commander." The Captain acknowledges, before turning back to pair of body-swapped time travellers. "As you have both probably concluded by now, there would seem to be absolutely nothing we can do to alter your predicament with the technology available to us but, as you are from the future, I need not tell you that!"

The Trusk - Bram - nods acceptance.

"Then what are we to do?" The human - Skyvyryk- splutters the words forth, unaccustomed as she is to the body which she now occupies, yet because she herself is a scientist from a more evolved age of her species, the Trusk, realises there is only logic up for consideration.

Captain Cirroc silently considers them both, not knowing the solution, nor what the best suggestion is to these two disparate characters, out of time and out of body.

"I can see only two options." The Captain says with a sigh, accepting total responsibility for what comes next, like the macho hero alpha he is. "We find an isolated area of space where nobody has followed us, and you both board Bram's ship, and leave amicably together. Or...we find the nearest penal colony and have you indefinitely incarcerated." He pauses. "The first option means you both have to reconcile yourselves with each other's feelings and experiences, that is, your future experience and the choice you both made to travel back in time. Plus there is the backward integration. The second option risks our own safety, which I shall accept, and you need not concern yourselves with any moralistic dilemma. That is to say the safety of my crew who are, by virtue of our life choices, which you, Bram...are aware of...because we are all renegades aboard the Sol Ship Excel."

Skyvyryk/Bram holds up a hand: "There is a third choice...euthanasia."

Bram/Skyvyryk is understandably confused: "What...is...that?"

"Not an option!" Captain Cirroc says forcefully.

Doctor Kelly D mutters: "I'm not so sure."

"Captain." Commander Mocha pipes up. "Might I offer an alternative."

"Not this time, Commander." Captain Cirroc says with yet another heroic, yet resigned sense of his own authority in this matter and, let's face, on the ship! "This decision must be equitable."

It all goes dramatically quiet in the infirmary, much like all good drama should - not that one likes to assume or presume!

Five days later and the Sol Ship Excel is proceeding on its journey to explore further unchartered space, visiting new planets and new life forms... unhindered by the constraints which Earth conformity forces upon the remaining fleet of vessels and its people.

Captain Cirroc sits at his chair watching the stars seemingly flash by as their speed dictates, but his mind is on the decision of Bram and Skyvyryk and the sacrifices they have made. His own choices still weigh heavily upon him, but that's why he is Captain of a ship in charge of numerous lives. Doctor Kelly D's ministrations offered only momentary distraction. The fate of the belligerent Trusk ship and the Sol Ship Bucktoo are unknown and their pursuit a distant memory.

Commander Mocha sits at her station behind the Captain, casting a glance at the back of his head. She says nothing. They have discussed the moral implications over the past five days, the meanings behind the decisions made, and messages of learning to be gained, a decision which was mutually debated but not necessarily universally agreeable.

Chief Engineer Mathilde Scobryne is monitoring the status of their engines and the power usage from her console on the bridge, rather than from the engine room, because her team are reliable. She, like the Doctor, has offered the necessary support to her Captain and does not envy his decision.

Lieutenant Z'Dar sits silently at the tactical console.

At the helm Lieutenant Chiwetel Jones is too focused on his job to think of anything else, afraid of everything yet competent and capable.

The elevator or lift door opens. Doctor Kelly D adjusts her uniform, making herself comfortable. She knows the Captain's hard…choices. The mental gymnastics which he fought over. The two choices he gave to the time travellers and their ultimate decision. She crosses the bridge, stands behind his chair, and puts a reassuring hand upon his shoulder.

"People need to learn to let things go, and squeeze the lemon the dry." Captain Cirroc says cryptically.

SPACE RENEGADES

EPISODE THREE

(Original script August 13th 1985)

'CONSPIRACY'

In the Captain's quarters onboard the Sol Ship Excel, Commander Ariana Mocha and Doctor Kelly D are partaking in a game with the Captain that doesn't include what your smutty mind is thinking! They sit in chairs around a circular table playing an epically famous, legendary board game from nineteen-eighties earth history called: THE Game. Everyone played it back then, and quite right too! This game involves accumulation of wealth, property, people, vehicles and the accoutrements which are no longer significant in this age of space travel. Why is this archaic, ancient board game still being played…who knows?

"Who will you swap for this person?" Captain Cirroc holds up a card for the Doctor to see, which features a long forgotten celebrity of insignificant importance from the twentieth century.

"I shall have to look." The Doctor responds.

"Don't take too long, Doctor." Commander Mocha says with irritation. "We haven't got all day!"

"Patience…," says the Doctor, "…is something of a virtue which you fail to possess."

Commander Mocha sighs impatiently, "Although I seldom see the point in playing this aimless, unproductive and distracting game which, I must add, a child of two years could master, I do appreciate its longevity and skill and the Captain's bewildering enjoyment of it. But…every time we play, Doctor, you unnecessarily take tediously pointless time making menial decisions."

"Sorry." Doctor Kelly D says unapologetically, looking with longing eyes at the Captain. "I will swap this person with you." The double entendre is unmistakable - or is it!?

They exchange cards.

Commander Mocha sighs from exasperation.

The panicked voice of Lieutenant Chiwetel Jones bursts forth from the shipboard intercom: "Bridge to Captain Cirroc!"

"I'm here, Lieutenant." The Captain calmly replies, much used to Jones's unnecessarily panicky tone.

"We are receiving a priority transmission from Admiral Picker, sir." The Lieutenants voice tells him from the ether.

Captain Cirroc exchanges curious glances with his fellow officers, saying to the air which would be mildly crazy if not for the communication: "Acknowledged, Lieutenant. I shall be along momentarily."

"Curious, Captain." Commander Mocha states with understatement. "Isn't Admiral Nastroil Picker Earth Station Gamma's commander?"

"That is correct, Commander." Captain Cirroc replies.

"What do you suppose he is doing out here, Captain. The last time we heard from him was…"

"I know, Commander, the exposition isn't required. Best we find out where he is, and what he wants."

Doctor Kelly D mutters: "Just as I was winning!"

Ten minutes later the trio are on the bridge of the Sol Ship, which is wisely placed at the centre of the ship, strongly fortified, rather than exposed at the front or top when any assault would annihilate the second most important part of a ship immediately, but what do I know!?

"Hi Captain." All the female bridge crew say at the same moment.

Commander Mocha sighs as she raises a hairless eyebrow, strokes her beard, and slides into the seat at her console.

Captain Cirroc strides to his chair, places both hands firmly on the back of it, and says, "Please put Admiral Picker on the view screen."

"Your wish…" Lieutenant Jones begins, deftly touching his console, and the image of Admiral Picker with his own bridge, appears large on the forward viewing screen.

"Hello, Captain Cirroc!" The Admiral's greeting is over friendly and forced, one might say. "It's a pleasure to see you so soon."

Captain Cirroc grins back cordially, "To what do we owe this splendiferous pleasure, Admiral?"

"Well, Captain," the Admiral says smilingly, "we have received a communication from our Earth Colony on the planet Zolpathica…one which I believe you are familiar with and, unless I am mistaken, is close to your present location?" Captain Cirroc hides any surprise he might have about how the Admiral, and the Earth Force itself, would know the present location of the Sol Ship Excel. "Anyway, their leader, Tru Daro, with whom I believe you are acquainted, is agreeable to finally begin negotiations regarding the planet's integration to our Earth Alliance."

"That does indeed sound jolly splendiferous, Admiral." Captain Cirroc's reply is sincere. "But why would you pick us of all ships? We are…self-confessed renegades, persecuted for our actions against the wayward beliefs of the Earth Alliance and, although aiding negotiations with the Zolpathica government certainly has an…appeal… you must admit, Admiral Picker, that picking us out does seem like a convenient trap."

Admiral Picker laughs somewhat awkwardly, his embarrassment evident. "I can fully understand your reticence, Captain. Were I in the same position as yourself and your crew, I undoubtedly would be suspicious too. But this is a genuine offer…and a request for your assistance. You have my complete assurance that there is no trap involved."

"Okay. Give me two minutes to discuss this proposal with my crew."

The image of Admiral Picker on the view screen is replaced with star scape.

"Opinions, please." The Captain says. "Apart from the obvious question about the Admiral's strangely obsequious attitude."

"C…Captain." Lieutenant Jones stammers. "How do they know where we are…and how can they communicate with us so easily?"

"Well…" The Captain begins but…

Commander Mocha butts in: "All Sol Ships are equipped with a transponder that cannot be disengaged without causing systemwide ship failure, Lieutenant. It is inconvenient to us as renegades, admittedly, and finding an alternate vessel would be the sensible thing to do if we are to fly freely and without Earth being aware of our location when we fly near to one of their outposts, which is clearly what we have somewhat foolishly done in this instance. But on this particular occasion it would seem a propitious mistake to ignore a historical event, such as presented by the Zolpathica alliance. It is safe to say that if this were in fact a trap, we are walking into it, but however, we would not be walking blindly. Our own goals are to further advance humanity and paint a positive image of Earth and human generally, to cultivate our civilisation. Therefore, I think we should proceed with this mission."

Doctor Kelly D mutters: "Strewth, give someone else a chance." She raises her voice. "I agree with the Commander."

"Sounds good to me, sir." Chief Scobryne offers. "I'm with you all the way, Captain!" No subtlety there!

Captain Cirroc nods, surveys the remainder of the bridge crew who offer no objections, and requests that Lieutenant Jones put the Admiral back on the view-screen.

"You picked the right people, Admiral." Captain Cirroc says.

"That's del…" The Admiral's image is replaced immediately by the star scape once more.

"Nicely done, Lieutenant." The Captain says. "That's a much more pleasant sight."

"Course plotted, sir."

"Splendiferous. Let's be on our way without any further ado, shall we?"

"Aye, aye, Captain!"

Commander Mocha addresses the Captain: "Might one enquire as to whom this Tru Daro of Zolpathica is, sir?"

"Of course." The Captain replies.

There's a long pause.

Doctor Kelly D sniggers: "It never gets old!"

"Zolpathica," begins Captain Cirroc, "is a mineral rich planet inhabited by the Zolpae, a race of humanoids much like ourselves with a few subtle cosmetic differences." Which makes them cheaper to present!? "Their culture reached a similar juncture to that which was on our twenty-first century earth, making them ideal for a colony to be situated there. Commander Douglas Bradley, Lieutenant Natasha Crawford, and myself introduced ourselves to the Zolpae leader some five years ago, when Earth was about exploration rather than defence and combat! They remained, I didn't, clearly. Tru Daro is still obviously in power, judging by Admiral Picker's statement."

"And our mission," commander Mocha says, "is to finalise the Zolpathica Earth alliance."

Chief Engineer Scobryne says, "Sounds simple enough."

"It should be." The Captain agrees. "Unless anything untoward has occurred during the intervening years."

Doctor Kelly D mutters, "Hmm, something's bound to go wrong!"

"Which is why," Captain Cirroc says, "you, Doctor, are going to lead the diplomatic team."

"But, Captain," Commander Mocha protests, "the good Doctor is barely diplomatic to her own patients!"

"In which case, this will be good experience."

"For once," says the Doctor, "I agree with the Commander."

"Choose your team wisely, Doctor. You have under three hours to prepare for this mission."

Three hours pass and Doctor Kelly D has her team assembled in the docking bay where Shuttle No. 13 awaits. Lieutenant Chiwetel Jones has already expressed his anxiety at the perceived unlucky shuttle number they are flying, but his doubt is quelled by Commander Mocha, who points out the lack of validity in the redundant ancient superstition. Lieutenant Z'Dar cheerfully carriers a shoulder bag which contains their equipment, while the fourth member of the team, a burly Ensign security officer - who clearly isn't coming back! - stands stoically awaiting orders.

"I have given your team a thorough briefing, Doctor." Commander Mocha says.

"I thought they looked bored!" The Doctor says.

"Good luck." The Commander offers.

"It'll be a piece of cake."

"A…what?" Lieutenant Z'Dar asks.

"An old earth expression, Lieutenant." Commander Mocha explains. "Which also means the good Doctor spends too much time in the company of our Captain!"

Without waiting for the anticipated reply, Commander Mocha turns on her heal and heads to the bridge, where the Zolpae leader, Tru Daro, is talking animatedly from the planets surface via the view-screen, or should that be vice versa?

"…truly splendiferous!" Laughs Daro, nodding. "I am correct? That is the word I heard you use numerous times upon our previous acquaintance?"

"Some might say too often, Daro." Captain Cirroc acknowledges, laughing also. "And it is very good to see you again, my old friend. I only wish that I could come down to Zolpathica myself, but alas, there are other more pressing matters which need my attention." Commander Mocha raises a quizzical hairless eyebrow. "But Daro, I am sending a worthy representative to conclude the negotiations in my good Doctor, Kelly D. Not only is she the best physician on my ship, but she is also a great diplomat."

A ripple of laughter cuts across the bridge.

"Excellent." Says Tru Daro naively! "When time permits, I shall confer with Douglas and Natasha, so you might speak with them."

"That would be splendiferous. It's a shame they're otherwise indisposed."

Tru Daro nods, "I look forward to speaking with you soon, Captain. Zolpathica out."

Shuttle No. 13 smoothly descends through the earth-like atmosphere of Zolpathica, the indistinct landmasses amidst three-quarters of the surface water taking on greater form and definition as they approach the central city of the Zolpae, located at the peak of a plateau on the main continent. Townships are scattered around the basin of the plateau, but the remainder of the planet is uninhabited by the Zolpae themselves, instead there is abundant flora and fauna, unlike on Earth where humans have sullied the land.

The city is low rise, mostly sun-bleached ochre buildings, and from above it appears a uniformly rich environment.

There is no obvious governmental office, nor are there buildings to satisfy status, but a section of a large rectangular green space has been partitioned off as a landing zone, which Lieutenant Jones finds, and sets the shuttle down upon without fanfare.

Commander Douglas Bradley and Tru Daro, plus entourage, greet the landing party once they disembark Shuttle No. 13.

"Welcome, friends." Daro's greeting is cordial.

"Thank you, Tru Daro." Doctor Kelly D extends her hand in the formal gesture. "I am Doctor Kelly D, chief medical officer of the Sol Ship Excel." She indicates her colleagues in turn, "This is Lieutenant Chiwetel Jones, Lieutenant Z'Dar, and a security guard whose name escapes me but I'm sure is of no great significance."

They all give Tru Daro the formal Zolpathica greeting except the stoic security guard - he is well aware of his place!

"Doctor!" Commander Douglas Bradley shakes Kelly D by the hand. "How's my old friend Xero?"

"That would be telling, Commander." Doctor D replies with a wink. "And you are Commander Bradley, I presume?"

"That's correct."

"I look forward to getting better acquainted, Commander."

Tru Daro clears his throat to get their attention: "Doctor. When we are amongst the citizens of Zolpathica and during these negotiations, may we refrain from being less formal and refer to each other by our first names? We prefer a more relaxed environment on Zolpathica that you on Earth."

"That sounds fine," Doctor D responds, "Tru."

"Ah…actually my first name is Daro. Sorry, I should've explained sooner."

The Doctor mutters: "Or Commander Mocha should've briefed us correctly! I know a little about your society, Daro, but I'm willing to learn more from you."

"Excellent." Tru Daro replies. "Douglas will give you a brief tour of this city while I attend to matters of state, and then we shall reconvene for dinner. If that suits yourself, Kelly?"

"Sounds perfect."

Tru Daro smiles ingratiatingly, before striding away with his entourage in tow.

"This way." Commander Douglas Bradley says.

They cross the lush healthy grass of the green space, the sky a clear blue green, the temperature a delightfully moderate warmth. The wall they approach is a rich brown, tightly packed with bricks, with ornamental etchings indigenous to the planet and its peoples.

They silently make their way through an arched aperture and down a narrow cobbled street, meeting nobody, until they reach a house which would be nondescript and indistinguishable from the rest of the street, were it not for a woven Earth Alliance banner hanging over its entrance. There is no door.

"This has been our…outpost, since our arrival all those years ago." Commander Bradley explains. "We have our workspace and sleeping quarters here, and have made it quite homely, really. You probably know that I have a team of six, including myself and Natasha…Lieutenant Crawford. This section of the city we are in is quite central, and the oldest part, like where you landed, but you probably noticed that already."

"Does your team have full access to facilities?" Lieutenant Z'Dar asks. "I'm studying multi-cultural dynamics, and the history of Zolpathica interests me greatly."

Commander Douglas Bradley nods.

"I'll arrange for a tour." The voice is that of Lieutenant Natasha Crawford. She has appeared in the entrance room of the Earth Outpost building. She smiles ingratiatingly. She is introduced to the new arrivals, "Welcome, all of you. How are you, Chiwetel?" She asks with familiarity.

"I'm, err…fine." Lieutenant Jones is visibly embarrassed in front of his colleagues - but, based upon the last two adventures, it's a surprise he doesn't burst into tears.

"You know each other?" Doctor D asks.

Lieutenant Jones blushes, "Yes."

"We go way back to the Academy on Earth." Natasha Crawford explains. "It's good to see you again, Chiwetel, we shall have to catch up when you're aligned."

"Doctor D, your task should be relatively easy." Commander states.

"That's a relief." The Doctor replies with… relief! "I'm not particularly…err…diplomatic! Ironic, I know, seeing that I'm a chief medical officer, but there you go, we cannot all be good at everything I suppose."

Natasha agrees. "I'll show you to your guest accommodation once you've had the tour of our Outpost." She says. "Daro has temporarily freed up a building behind us for you. There's a square with an ornamental garden between that and the Outpost. It's quite lovely." To Chiwetel, "Like back at the Academy, where we had our breakfast liaisons."

Lieutenant Jones's blushes deepen, and Commander Bradley takes this as his cue to show them around the Outpost.

On the Sol Ship Excel's bridge, the crew go about their regular tasks, only now Commander Mocha is monitoring all space traffic communications with added efficiency, and Captain Cirroc is seated at a console next to her checking numerous information from across the ship, and from Zolpathica.

"Captain." Says Commander Mocha. "I am still…unsettled by the decision to send Doctor D on this assignment." She strokes her beard thoughtfully. "Kelly is a fine medical professional, that is unquestionable, and I acknowledge that at face value the relative simplicity of these negotiations in their present form leave little room for errors of judgement, but this is the Doctor! Her patience couldn't be described as diplomatic."

"Agreed. But what could possibly go wrong in a couple of days?"

"With the Doctor…two days could see the total annihilation of the Zolpae!"

Captain Cirroc laughs, "I agree that based upon some of her past choices the Doctor might be seen as a questionable…choice, but I have faith in her and, like you say, these negotiations are pretty much done and dusted so there's really nothing to worry about."

"That's why I'm worried."

The Captain sighs, "Anyway, Commander, have you detected anything out there which might pose a threat…not to the negotiations, but to us?"

"Not yet, Captain."

"That's good. Everything shipboard is shipshape, too! What could possibly go wrong?"

"I hesitate to remind you, Captain, by stating that, my anxiety rises exponentially!"

At 1800 - Zolpathica time - Kelly D, Jones and Z'Dar are seated next to Douglas and Natasha at a circular wooden table on the edge of the field where their shuttle is parked - don't worry about the security guard, he will be fine. Tru Daro and half a dozen Zolpae representatives sit opposite, the scant clothing looking positively informal compared to the uniforms of the three newcomers.

The evening air is warm, the sky bright and blue and idyllic. An assortment of foods colourfully adorn the table upon ceramic plates, drinks in jugs, and eating utensils of a familiar sort. The setting couldn't be any more perfect, what could possibly go wrong?

Tru Daro introduces the representatives to the guests, ending with the nearest Zolpae: "Dre Bollatistio is my senior advisor." The tall female of the species stands, bows very slowly, and after ten minutes of this she sits. Tru Daro lifts up his half-full mug in a toast, "On behalf of the Zolpae people, we offer our sincere greetings to our guests and hope these negotiations reach a speedy, mutually agreeable resolution. Personally, I hope you enjoy your stay with us. Also…we should thank the fruitful labourers who toiled and tended the earth to provide us with a bountiful meal, our humble appreciation for their work should not be underestimated."

They each raise a mug in thanks, drinking a mouthful of the sweet, fruity nectar offered.

Then, they eat in respectful and ritualistic silence until the food has been completely consumed, and the table cleared away, the drink remaining.

Doctor Kelly D stands and, for once, doesn't mutter, "On behalf of myself and my colleagues, I thank you for your kindness and generosity. Your food, although unfamiliar to us, was exquisite." The Doctor raises her mug, takes a sip, and seats herself.

Dre Bollatistio stands and addresses them, "You honourably deserve acknowledgment for respecting our culture. Thank you." She drinks from her mug before reseating herself.

"I concur." Tru Daro says, bowing. "We believe that a long time ago, far, far away, a race known to lore as Gatherers plucked our ancestors from our original home-world, placing them on Zolpathica to further our race. It is believed that our society evolved over many hundreds of years, until great wars devastated our planet owing to the greed and lack of willpower of…others. Through sheer desperation and determination, over much time those who remained reconnected and committed to forging a better world, one where technology would be used minimally and the land unsullied by our unnatural creations. Our city here, and the small outlying communities, harmoniously sustain us and world around us."

The Zolpae murmur their agreement, taking a sip from their drink. The guests follow suit.

Lieutenant Z'Dar stands up, looks around nervously, before saying, "I…admire how you have been able to integrate technology into your society, especially after what your ancestors did…which is not too dissimilar to my own people, or that on Earth, as I understand from my studies." The Lieutenant sits back down, unsure whether he has exceeded protocol.

Commander Bradley stands, addressing Tru Daro, "I have promised to show young Z'Dar here as much of your culture as time permits. He is presently studying multi-dynamics." He explains.

"A most admirable choice." Tru Daro bows his head in acknowledgement. "Please feel free, young Z'Dar, to explore our city as is your own pleasure. You will find we Zolpae like nothing more than to share our knowledge and experiences."

Lieutenant Z'Dar grins.

Dre Bollatistio stands, addressing Lieutenant Z'Dar. "You might also be interested to learn the hierarchical structure of our society. Daro is our nominated leader, which the prefix Tru signifies. As the Dre signifies my position. All citizens are equal. Work is equally divided. People choose their jobs and lives. Our government is an appointment and based on a flexible system, which takes greater responsibility for the wellbeing of our citizens and culture. There is no corrupting power-base which is often found in many other cultures. We all work to provide for others while collectively expanding our knowledge and appreciation of the land around us. Our desires are attuned significantly differently to those on other planets. Although our system would by no means be perfect for adaption, it is well worth understanding." She sits.

Tru Daro stands, "Tomorrow I shall assign you a guide, Z'Dar. Someone experienced in the work you study. They will show you many facets of our culture which I'm certain you will find fascinating."

"Thank you." Lieutenant Z'Dar bows his head respectfully.

"Are there any further questions? Asks Tru Daro, who is greeted by silence. "In which case, I shall draw this meal to a close by offering our thanks once more to the providers of the food and drink, and may their endeavours bring further pleasure to the people."

They all silently leave the table, as is customary on Zolpathica. When the three newcomers and their colleagues are beyond the wall and walking the cobblestone street toward the Outpost, the silence is broken.

Natasha takes hold of Lieutenant Jones's elbow. "Breakfast tomorrow morning in the courtyard, Chiwetel. It will be like old times."

"Err, yes, of course." The Lieutenant replies, trying to avoid the glances of curiosity he receives from the others. "I would like that."

"You're in for a fun day tomorrow, Z'Dar." Commander Bradley says. "The Zolpathica and their culture are truly unique."

"Thank you, Comm…Bradley." Z'Dar offers.

Doctor Kelly D mutters, "Great. You guys have fun while I'm stuck in negotiations." She shrugs with resignation.

They all retire to their rooms.

Doctor Kelly D reports in to the Sol Ship Excel.

"How's it going, Doctor?" The voice of the Captain sounds from the ether - you know the drill!

"So far, so good, Captain. Our first formal gathering went well, and their food and drink is so fresh it's delicious. I am to begin finalising negotiations tomorrow, with the conclusion the day after, apparently. Also, it seems Lieutenant Jones has prior acquaintance with Lieutenant Crawford, not that it's anything to worry about, but he will be occupied tomorrow. And Lieutenant Z'Dar is going to be shown around some of the Zolpathica sights. Seems like we might be here a couple of days."

"Sounds like you're having fun." The Captain comments.

The Doctor mutters, "They are!"

"We have nothing unusual to report up here, Doctor. It seems our Earth Alliance friends are being true to their word. Well, anyway, be careful…Kelly. Don't take anything for granted. And good luck."

"Thank you, Captain."

A beautiful cascade of morning sunshine casts dark shadows and silhouettes along the alleyways of the Zolpathican city. The sky is golden and blue, the air warm. Colourful small birds herald in the beginning of a new day, some darting across the tops of the low-rise buildings. Other indigenous animals call and coo.

At a small wooden table in the middle of the courtyard, between the Outpost and quarters of the four members of the Sol Ship Excel, sit Lieutenants Chiwetel Jones and Natasha Crawford. An assortment of morning food and drink, like breakfast - only of the alien version - have been brought to them.

"…the Appollician Falls on the Northern ascent of the plateau are beautiful." Concludes Natasha, sipping a syrupy beverage with the consistency of coffee. "I've already mentioned them to your Doctor, Kelly D, and she says it's fine for me to borrow you for most of the day." She says.

"That sounds…err…fine." Chiwetel offers nervously, but he's always nervous because it's his natural tendency to be so, which everyone who knows him is well aware of and aren't judgmental towards. "How long…err…how long will it take to get there?"

"About an hour on foot. Walking is the only way of things in the city environments. The Zolpathica have space faring machines, of course, but they're on the eastern edge of the city, away from the general population and their surroundings."

Chiwetel is hesitant to respond. "Isn't that… err…a bit inconvenient. I mean, I don't want to… you know…but don't people here…the Zolpae… want to explore space?"

"Sure they do. But this culture here is much different to that which you and I are accustomed to in so many ways. Let's finish up, and I can give you more detail on our journey."

Chiwetel nods his consent.

Dre Bollatistio and Lieutenant Z'Dar are walking through a long, wide treelined boulevard between low-rise homes where Zolpae residents are going about their early morning chores.

"Dre is a prefix," Bollatistio explains, "denoting my position as Tru Daro's second, as it were. Before this I was known as Dac, which means technician. That was my chosen vocation, and one which I continue and shall return to once my present position changes in two years time."

Lieutenant Z'Dar nods. "And Bor are land farmers?"

"That's correct. They specialise in providing sustenance, although each and everyone of us participate in farming on a minimum level."

"How do you prevent things like avarice and ego from happening?"

"They are human concepts which I have learned existed in our past also. They aided in the destruction of our ancestors. We have found a balance in our lives which preserve the values and principles of everyone, yet do not curtail our desires to achieve more aspirations."

"Is that why you are now ready to join the Earth Alliance?"

"Yes." Dre Bollatistio replies hesitantly. "Although there are some dissenting voices, but that is to be expected in any culture."

Doctor Kelly D and the nameless security guard make their way up a narrow street to the walled green space, site of the evening meal, and resting place for Shuttle No. 13. The dining table has been randomly repositioned for no apparent reason, and has jugs of drink with accompanying mugs upon it. Tru Daro and a duo from last nights pleasantries are awaiting them.

The Doctor mutters, "This'll be fun!"

Before the security guard can comment, Tru Daro rises from the table and greets them in the formal hug and kisses - weirdo!

"Let the negotiations," Tru Daro says at great length, "commence."

They sit silently at the table because, apparently the negotiations are a long and drawn out affair which requires much thinking - yawn!

On the bridge of the Sol Ship Excel the morning shift is beginning for its crew. Captain Cirroc steps out of the lift or elevator, stretching and yawning, a young female Ensign in his wake. She smiles demurely yet knowingly at the Captain - well, who can blame her, he is pretty irresistible - before taking up a position at the tactical station at which Lieutenant Z'Dar usually sits.

Commander Mocha raises her hairless eyebrow, having noted the exchange between her Captain and the Ensign. She strokes her beard disapprovingly.

"Good morning, everyone!" Captain Cirroc says cheerfully.

Before anyone can reply a warning siren blares out, the red alert comes on, and HEAL - the Hologram Emitting Artificial Lifeform - computer springs into being.

"Sol Ship Bucktoo detected, Captain!" The computer announces. "Approaching from sector nineteen. Defensive shields up! Suggest we beat a hasty retreat if we want to remain renegades!"

"I agree with the computer, Captain!" Commander Mocha agrees!

"Engineering to Bridge!" It's Chief Scobryne on the air! "Full power available! What's going on! Are we under attack!? I've not had breakfast yet!" Adding more calmly, "But you would know that already, Captain!"

Commander Mocha rolls her eyes.

"Calm down, everyone." Captain Cirroc says… calmly. "HEAL…stand down alert. Commander Mocha…lower our shields and monitor the Bucktoo's course. Chief Engineer Scobryne…get some breakfast, everything's fine. Ensign Lefler… could you try contacting the Bucktoo for me please?"

Ensign Lefler turns about in her seat, brushes the hair from her eyes, wantonly looking at the Captain before replying: "Yes, sir."

Seconds later and Admiral Picker's face appears abruptly on the main viewing screen.

"Hello, Captain!" The Admiral says with nauseating excitement. "How are things going with the negotiations?"

"Splendiferously thank you, Admiral." Replies Captain Cirroc. "My representative should be conducting the negotiations as we speak."

"Good, good."

"You know, Admiral, you gave my crew a bit of a fright by arriving unannounced like this. They were under the impression that you might be conspiring to capture us."

Admiral Picker laughs. "Not at all, Captain, not at all. Please assure them we shall not approach. We have arrived a bit sooner than expected, that's all."

"Fair enough. Cirroc out."

Admiral Picker's face is replaced by the more appealing image of the planet Zolpathica.

"Captain." Says Commander Mocha. "Might I point out that the arrival of Admiral Picker and the Bucktoo might be considered a portent for our probable capture. As discussed prior to our undertaking this assignment, the Earth Alliance want these Zolpathica negotiations to proceed with us heading them, consequently detaining us here for a prolonged period of time. Admiral Picker's prompt arrival would mean a conspiracy against us, as you suggested, sir. I would strongly recommend we leave as soon as possible."

Captain Cirroc nods thoughtfully. "It will take more than the Admiral to bring us in, Commander. Find a way for HEAL to communicate with the Bucktoo's computer, and try to extend our sensors range by utilising theirs."

"Yes, Captain."

"For the present time, we shall trust the Admiral's claim. As soon as we hear from our people on Zolpathica, we can instruct them accordingly. These negotiations are far too important for Picker to jeopardise them by interfering."

Cascading water from the Appollician Falls boom and crash into the misty basin hundreds of feet below. Lieutenant Chiwetel Jones and Lieutenant Natasha Crawford observe the spectacle from afar.

"This...this reminds me of Niagara." Chiwetel says.

"Brings back memories." Natasha agrees.

"It does."

Natasha chuckles, "Memories of you jumping in!"

She leads him along a descending trail.

"Gravity jumping wasn't my idea!" Chiwetel says. "It was Doug's."

"Yes. And he wouldn't do it now, either."

"You mean…?"

"Sure. But I haven't brought the equipment with me today."

"I was… I would do anything for you…back in day."

"And I, you. But things change. Life moves on. All the usual cliches, really!"

"Are you and Doug…?"

Natasha laughs, "No. Definitely not. He's too much of the jealous type for my taste, not to mention childish. Fate threw us together on Zolpathica, nothing more."

"He hasn't…barely said a word to me since I got here."

"Doug is a busy man. He's committed to his work here. Don't think anything of it. And like I said…he's childish in many ways."

They reach the bottom of the basin, walking along the riverbank until the raging water of the falls begins to calm. Natasha puts her hand into Chiwetel's.

"I'm sorry it didn't work out, Chiwetel." She says. "I'm proud of you for standing with Captain Cirroc, although I don't approve of your choice to exist as a…renegade from the Earth Alliance. It's a shame that we human's have mostly reverted to the old ways, the hateful ways."

"They seem to be trying to integrate here, though. The alliance with Zolpathica. I mean… Captain Cirroc seems to think it's a genuine thing."

Natasha nods, "Maybe it is. These people don't necessarily have any technology which could be exploited. So…maybe…who knows ?" They stop. "Anyway…fancy taking a swim?"

Doctor Kelly D sits at the negotiating table waiting for the trio of Zolpae to respond to her latest question, given to her during the discussions held between Captain Cirroc and the crew of Excel before her departure. She resists drumming her fingers on the table or tutting impatiently. She tries not to think of her neglected duties onboard the Excel. She tries not to think of Xero! But it's a difficult challenge!

It is now late afternoon and Kelly is getting hungry. She doesn't need a clock to tell her the time. She hopes they will stop soon for a break and some food. She's drunk enough, taken toilet breaks, but even in the future a stomach will grumble if empty. The non-essential security guard departed a while ago to use the toilet and hasn't returned. Maybe he is having a sneaky sandwich somewhere! Lucky him.

She also feels it necessary to report to the Excel what has transpired thus far, which in truth seems to be very little, but as there's little to finalise Kelly D isn't at all surprised.

After what seems to be an extraordinarily long process, Tru Daro eventually speaks, "That is enough discussion for today, I think, Doctor. My colleagues and I are entirely satisfied with the proposals your Earth Alliance have suggested, and tomorrow morning we shall formally make our pledge to your organisation."

Doctor Kelly D smiles with not a small amount of relief that this will all be over soon, and she can return to the ship. This diplomatic stuff is beyond her remit. She does wonder what these Zolpae individuals would think if she told them her Captain and vessel were renegades, being chased down by the Earth Alliance but asked to carry out this job as a favour!

"There will be a celebration dinner tonight." Tru Daro states.

They all stand, bow and depart the table.

Doctor Kelly D walks across the soft grass, pleased to be stretching her legs. The sun and blue sky are very inviting, and she will ask their hosts at the Outpost where the nearest bath-house can be found. She could do with a soak and a massage and any other service these people can provide.

Commander Douglas Bradley intercepts the Doctor before she reaches the Outpost. His expression is grave.

"Hello Commander, what's wrong?" The Doctor asks.

"There's been a murder." He explains at length.

On the bridge of the Sol Ship Excel everyone is attending to the routines of a spaceship. Captain Cirroc exits the lift or elevator, straightening his shirt. He too has been tending to ship routines by checking up on the various departs and making sure everything is running smoothly and shipshape - yes, really, the future isn't entirely about fun adventure stuff, although of course our Captain's irresistibility means his work and play ratio fluctuates greatly.

The Captain crosses the bridge to his chair, sitting down, grinning at a thought, unseeing eyes on the view screen, mind elsewhere.

"Captain!" Commander Mocha says. "We are being contacted by Doctor D."

"Splendiferous." Says the Captain, tapping a button on his armchair console which opens up communications between himself and the Doctor. "Good afternoon, Doctor! How are things proceeding with the negotiations?"

"They are fine, Captain." The Doctor replies. "But that's not what I'm calling about. It's Lieutenant Jones, sir…"

"Out with it, Doctor, the suspense is killing us up here."

"Lieutenant Jones has been accused by the Zolpae of murdering Lieutenant Natasha Crawford this afternoon."

There is a collective intake of shocked breath from the bridge crew.

Captain Cirroc stands up, tightly holding the armrests of his chair - not for dramatic purposes, you understand! "What happened?" He asks.

Doctor Kelly D tells the Captain that Lieutenant's Jones and Crawford spent the morning and early afternoon together, returning to the Outpost, shortly after which the unimportant security officer found the body of Lieutenant Crawford - she had been dispatched with by a sharp implement, as yet unknown and undiscovered by the local authorities.

"Okay." Captain Cirroc acknowledges with great distraction, assessing the information. "Is there visual information to go on?"

"Negative, sir." The Doctor's voice replies from the ether. "The Zolpae possess no surveillance capabilities whatsoever. Our security person whatshername is aiding the locals in their investigation."

"Thank you."

"Captain!" Commander Mocha says somewhat more calmly than the exclamation mark might signify. "Tru Daro is trying to contact us."

"On screen."

"Not yet!"

Captain Cirroc sighs, "I always fall for that!"

The face of Tru Daro appears upon the viewing screen as if by magic, although it's not magic, it's technology. The Zolpae representatives face is full of solemnity, although they are are relatively solemn people, so it's impossible to distinguish between expressions.

"Daro." The Captain says. "I've just heard the tragic news. I trust my security officer is aiding your investigation to the best of her ability, but if there is any further assistance I might offer, please do not hesitate to ask."

"Xero," says Tru Daro, "that is very gracious of you. Might I also offer my own sincere regrets that such a tragedy should occur on this most momentous occasion, and I hope that no aspersions shall be made regarding the circumstances."

"Not at all, Daro."

"Tomorrow will see the signing of our treaty and the resolution of this situation."

"That sounds perfectly splendiferous."

The image of Tru Daro is replaced by the planet Zolpathica and a star scape, as if by magic, only not magic!

"This is an unexpected event." Captain Cirroc announces with understatement.

Commander Mocha strokes her beard and raises her hairless eyebrows, "I admit that I expected the Doctor to mess up these negotiations which, on face value, seemed simple to execute. Yet…drama seems to accompany us on our journey, Captain, so one should never be surprised that something has occurred to unbalance the situation. Shall I contact Admiral Picker and update him on this matter?"

"You must be joking."

"You should be well aware by now, Captain, that I never joke about my work."

"Quite so, and I apologise for even the slightest offence caused, but no, I do not wish you to tell Admiral Picker that one of my crew has possibly murdered someone, thank you!"

"Do I detect…sarcasm, Captain!?"

Doctor Kelly D and the security guard, who you assumed incorrectly was going to die pretty quickly, are standing in the main room of the Outpost with Commander Douglas Bradley, the Zolpae investigation director, and Tru Daro.

"I have dispatched a messenger," Tru Daro is saying, "to locate Bollatistio and Z'Dar. Just as a precaution. Whomever it was that has framed

Chiwetel for Natasha's murder, and whomever they are working with, might not know that we know that they did this, and might cause more unrest against this alliance with Earth."

Doctor Kelly D nods, "I understand why you want to confine these facts and the new evidence presented by your investigation director, Daro, to the five of us…but I think it only appropriate that I should inform my Captain."

"Later, friend Kelly." Tru Daro holds up his hands in a placating manner. "After our celebration dinner this evening. Beforehand, I would like to request that my investigation director and your security guard work together, and observe any untoward behaviour tonight. I want to see if they cannot root out the perpetrators of this heinous crime before the signing of the treaty tomorrow."

"As you wish."

Commander Bradley speaks up, "I trust your people implicitly, Daro, and if this is the beginning of a protracted insurrection by those opposed to your administration agreeing to this alliance with Earth, then I'm sure Captain Cirroc will understand the need for discretion. We have at our disposal technology which can better protect the delegates tonight, and with your permission I should feel safer if they were in place."

Tru Daro deliberates the proposal. "As long as those measures aren't likely to cause the perpetrators to be forewarned."

"You have my personal assurance," says the Commander, "that nobody will suspect a thing."

"In which case, Douglas, please make them so."

They disperse.

Doctor Kelly D walks by herself to the deserted open green space. Her purpose and mind is made up. She strides towards Shuttle No.13 as if inspecting its condition. Tapping her shoulder communicator as discretely as possible, Kelly contacts the Sol Ship Excel and Captain Cirroc, telling him in detail what has transpired since last they spoke, their future plans, and precautions - ooh, exciting stuff,

That evening the humans and Zolpae representatives converge on the ancient table set for the meal. Commander Bradley and Doctor Kelly D are first to arrive - the security guard from the Excel and chief security officer of the Zolpae, sit in a room to monitor the terrorist prevention measures from the opposite side of the wall.

Three formally attired Zolpae from the council arrive next, followed by Dre Bollatistio and Tru Daro.

They are all standing with the solemnity one might expect for such an important event.

"Welcome, one and all." Tru Daro says. He goes on to extol and expound upon the virtues and ideals which have come from the past experiences suffered by the Zolpae, culminating in this moment, and tomorrow's historical events - basically, it's all very political hyperbole and hypocrisy to excite the masses, never mind those dissidents and factions which might be considered terrorist - blah, blah, blah!

Everyone present nods with due respect and dignity.

After more 'politician speak' from Tru Daro, the meal commences in respectful silence, with sounds of nature their only accompaniment - the city is at rest while this dignified scene takes place, mostly.

Towards the meals conclusion and from a far corner of the great green expansion, there is movement. A flutter of banners. Ten Zolpae citizens, protesters and insurgents, chanting their slogans, are approaching the delegates at the table.

Doctor Kelly D is the first to notice their presence, having received a secret communication from the Excel security guard. She raises the alarm.

In the room behind the wall, the Zolpae security chief draws the razor sharp blade of a ceremonial knife across the throat of the Excel security guard. He turns a dial on the retrofitted computer panel at the desk before him, touches a communication button and says with relish: "The shield is down."

The delegation from Zolpae turn their heads. Commander Bradley and Doctor Kelly D rise from their seats.

Across the grass expanse the chanting gains in volume as the rowdy protestors approach.

Doctor D taps her shoulder communicator, "Scan for weapons." And seconds later the computer voice of HEAL replies, "No weapons detected."

Commander Bradley says, "Daro. I'm sure they're harmless. They're just unarmed protesters. But to be on the safe side…?"

"Call in the security detail." Tru Daro says with resignation to the Commander's unspoken suggestion then, to his fellow Zolpae, "Stay where you are. We are all quite safe."

The delegates exchange glances, eventually nodding at the command of their leader. Dre Bollatistio is watching the approaching protestors calmly.

Doctor Kelly D moves away from the table, eyes scanning the wall as far as she can see. The shield will protect the delegates as long as none of them wander. Tru Daro has made certain they won't. There is no untoward motion.

From the wall archway the Zolpae security chief emerges with six of his officers. They are armed with photonic laser guns.

But the non-appearance of the unnamed Excel security guard causes Doctor Kelly D concern. The plan was that he should stick with them at all times.

The Doctor taps her shoulder communicator, "HEAL." She says in a hushed tone, like when she mutters! "Is the shield still up?"

The reply is instant, "Negative, Doctor."

"Active Kelly One!"

Nothing visibly occurs, but the Doctor knows the shuttles protection shield has extended around the table and those within its proximity. This precaution wasn't her doing. Captain Cirroc had suggested it on the outside chance that something like this might happen. He had reasoned that nobody could know how deeply this insurrection was embedded within the Zolpae civilisation, so nobody should be trusted. The Excel security guard's absence could only mean one thing at this point!

Instead of pointing weapons at the approaching protesters, the security detail rake aim at the delegates.

"What's the meaning of this!?" Barks Tru Daro.

"HEAL. Neutralise threat!" The Doctor says calmly.

A red beam lances out from Shuttle No.13, crossing the distance across the green expanse in under a second, lacing the security detail in a neutralising energy field which causes them to stop abruptly in their tracks. The security Zolpae chief tries activating his weapon but nothing happens. They are helplessly trapped.

The protesters cease their forward movement, gathering themselves in, waiting to see what will next transpire.

The entrance door to Shuttle No.13 hisses as it opens, the ramp descends, and out march six Sol Ship Excel security officers, who run up-to the Zolpae security team and surround them. The Zolpae drop their weapons in surrender.

"What…?" Tru Daro is confused.

"Don't worry, Daro." Says Doctor D. "Everything is under control, now." She taps her shoulder communicator, "HEAL. Shield and stasis field down."

The energy beam retreats and the Zolpae traitors are taken into custody.

Commander Douglas Bradley has removed himself from the delegates, who congratulate themselves on a resounding victory and satisfying resolution. Their pretentiously cheerful placating, obsequious manner, has sickened him to the core for the last time. His likeminded Zolpae friends in the insurgency have been sacrificed accordingly. They have been captured by the blinkered men who cannot see beyond the pale history of their own lives. Douglas has also sacrificed. The murder of Lieutenant Natasha Jones was not easy. Not just the act itself, or implicating her old acquaintance and beau, Lieutenant Jones. But the difficulty in accepting the young woman's sacrifice. Douglas loved Natasha. Always had, always would. But that love had been repeatedly denied.

The Commander draws out the weapon he secreted in his clothing, "For the cause!" He shouts somewhat fanatically and squeezes the trigger…

Nothing happens.

Doctor Kelly D calmly removes the weapon from his impotent grip, "Sorry, Commander, but our motto is 'hope for the best, prepare for the worst.'"

The Commander's shoulders slump defeatedly.

On the bridge of the Sol Ship Excel with everything resolved and tied up in a neat bow - good grief, it does get worse! - Lieutenant Chiwetel Jones, at the helm, plots a course away from the planet Zolpathica. Lieutenant Z'Dar has a faraway, rueful expression upon his alien face - he has enjoyed discovering the culture of the Zolpae, has learned much, and will miss the company of them. Doctor Kelly D stands with a sardonic smile by the open lift, or elevator, door - mission accomplished. Commander Ariana Mocha strokes her beard, thoughtfully watching the receding planet as they leave it, and the story, behind them.

Captain Cirroc sits rigidly in his chair, a pensive expression upon his face. He is not entirely sure if their mission by proxy was successful. The Earth Alliance has gained another world into their collective, yes. But he isn't entirely convinced their motives were truly altruistic.

Thus…the bridge crew are silent, caught up in their own thoughts, boldly going into their next adventure, forever changed.

SPEC SCRIPT FOR STAR TREK DEEP SPACE NINE

I have included in this collection the following Star Trek Deep Space Nine story which I sent off to the producers at Paramount Studios - at the time, they would look at a maximum of two unsolicited scripts sent to them by the same author.

My script was evidently shown some modicum of interest because after an eight month wait, I had it returned to me with a covering letter, upon which were three individual dates and signatures scrawled upon its cover - I like to think three script-readers passed it along for consideration, but maybe it's just my own flight of fancy!

Despite the rejection I have retained my script, the return covering letter from Paramount Pictures, and the envelope, for posterity.

I have presented this story here in its original format with a few minor omissions and cosmetic alterations.

Star Trek
Deep Space Nine

"Day of Reckoning"

Submitted to Paramount early in 1997.
Last log date stamp by Lolita Fatjo at Paramount November 14th 1997.

TEASER:

1   Interior DS9 Corridor.

Close-up on the boots of Worf and Odo at they match each others stride.

2   Interior Detention Block.

Laying stretch out on a cell bunk in K'Lonth Bidar - a Klingon female in her early years. She casually wears a colourful flowing gown and ornate jewellery.

Work and Odo enter, stopping just outside the cell.

Bidar regards them and smiles before she pushes herself into a sitting position, swiping her flowing hair back from her face.

BIDAR- Good afternoon. (Her voice is soft.) I cannot tell you what a pleasure it is to be visited by the two most eligible men on this station. No doubt you have come to apologise for your mistake confining me here. (Seductively.) Or perhaps you are going to me why I have been sitting here alone for the past two hours?

WORF- (snarling) K'Lonth Bidar, have you no honour? You are a disgrace to the Empire! Those clothes and cheap jewellery do you no favour! A true warrior would not wear such trappings!

BIDAR- (laughing) All that from a Klingon warrior dressed in a Starfleet uniform! How pretentious can someone be! And as for insulting my appearance...I did not hear your complaints upon our first acquaintance. In fact I was only allowed on this station because you authorised it!

WORF- Two oversights which I am now regretting.

Odo gives Worf a sideways glance eye-roll.

BIDAR- (to Odo) Constable Odo. Maybe you can tell me why the strong arms of the law hauled me in here? Or do I have to continue listening to Worf's... inadequacies?

ODO- Where were you at precisely oh-five-hundred hours this morning, Miss Bidar?

BIDAR- That's easy...I was with the Doctor.

WORF- (disgusted) Julian Bashir!?

ODO- I presume it was a medical visit?

BIDAR- Certainly not! I'm in prime physical health! As is Julian for a human, I must say. (To Worf) The Doctor is more virile than some Klingon's I could mention!

Worf snarls.

ODO- (quickly) You were with the Doctor all night?

BIDAR- Definitely. I count myself fortunate that not medical emergencies arose.

Worf's jaw works furiously with apoplexy. Bidar winks teasingly.

ODO- Miss Bidar! Do I take it you were not engaged in business on docking pylon three at oh-five-hundred hours this morning?

BIDAR- I was not, my dear Constable Odo. Sorry. As I have already explained to you and Worf, I was engaged in business with Doctor Bashir. Unless you require more detail?

ODO- I believe that you have made the picture adequately clear, for the Commander and myself.

WORF- (to Bidar) Why are you lying to us, K'Lonth Bidar? We have a witness who can place you on docking pylon three at precisely the time in question!

BIDAR- And Commander, I am positive that if you ask Julian he will corroborate my alibi! What is the accusation? Or shall I guess? Murder! Who have I been accused of killing now?

WORF- You do not know who your victim was?

ODO- Murder is just one of the crimes under investigation, Miss Bidar, for which you are presently our prime suspect. (To Worf.) Except for Quark, he is always a suspect.

WORF- K'Lonth Bidar! Why did you murder the Bajoran criminal, Ular Smoug?

BIDAR- I have not murdered anyone, Commander…at least, not recently!

WORF- Why did you sabotage a Virbitin cruiser?

BIDAR- (laughing) I have not been near your docking pylon, Commander! You are making a big mistake and wasting your time! The real murderer and saboteur is probably making their escape! I thought you knew me better, Commander Worf?

ODO- If we are wrong, Miss Bidar, then I will offer my profound apology. But in the meantime I am confining you here under suspicion of the aforementioned murder and sabotage, which resulted in the death of Major Kira Nerys.

FADE OUT.

ACT ONE:

3   Interior Ops.

Sisko is leaning with his back against the central circular control table, at which both Dax and O'Brien are seated.

SISKO-   (massaging his brow) Play it again for me, Dax.

DAX-   Alright, Benjamin, but it hasn't altered since last time.

SISKO-   Pity!

4   Exterior Space and DS9.

A scissor-shaped Virbitin cruiser detached from pylon three. A runabout approach it. The Virbitin ship explodes and vaporises the runabout.

5   Interior Ops.

Sisko screws his eyes shut, rubbing them before facing the control table once more - the image is frozen on the explosion.

SISKO- Did it really happening so quickly? Did the Major not have time to give the Virbitin cruiser a wider berth? Why were they allowed to pass so closely?

O'BRIEN- Dax and I have been trying to answers those questions for the past twelve hours, Captain. We cannot find any fault with the station's sensors. Everything this end was operating within the correct parameters. I hate to admit it, sir, but it looks like it was a freak accident which neither the Virbitin cruiser, or Major Kira's runabout, could've avoided.

SISKO- Are you positive that sabotage was involved?

DAX- That's something we do know, Benjamin. It's very clear from the recording that the Virbitin's engines exploded with significant force to indicate foul play. And we have the dead Bajoran on pylon three who was definitely murdered!

O'BRIEN- It's fortunate for us we have an eye witness.

SISKO- But it's unfortunate that our suspect in the Klingon woman! Have you heard anything from Worf or Odo?

DAX- Nothing yet. They let her simmer in her cell for a couple of hours. I'm confident that with them working together than anybody, even a

Klingon, would think twice before spinning a false story of denial.

SISKO- (sighing with exasperation) Let us hope it was her and that she does confess, because I feel much safer with a saboteur locked up! Have we had any trouble from other ships wanting to leave the station?

O'BRIEN- No, sir. Trade has been slack these past few days. None of the ships that are here are in a hurry to leave.

DAX- Benjamin. Can I offer some advice?

SISKO- Always, old man.

DAX- May I recommend you get some rest? (Smiling) You've been awake for almost thirty-six hours and look tired.

SISKO- Wise advice, old man!

DAX- Absolutely, Benjamin. Captain Yates's ship docked yesterday, and I presume you had much to talk about?

SISKO- (smiling ruefully) She was only here for a twenty-four hour layover, old man, so yes we did have a lot of talking to do.

O'BRIEN- We will inform you straight away if we make any new discoveries, Captain. (Muttering) Although I can't see what!

SISKO- Thank you, Chief. My first officer is dead, and I want to know why!

6 Interior Infirmary.

Doctor Bashir presses a hypo-spray against the arm of Ensign Karen Ash and injects the drug.

BASHIR- You'll be as right as rain come tomorrow, Ensign Ash.

ASH- Thank you Julian. I can call you Julian, can't I?

BASHIR- I wouldn't want it any other way, Ensign.

She hopped off the medical table just as Odo and Worf enter. They wait just inside the door.

ASH- I don't know how I can thank you for all the help you have been able to give me, Julian. Perhaps you might allow me to buy you a drink at Quark's sometime?

BASHIR- That would be nice, Ensign. Thank you.

ASH- How about tonight?

BASHIR- That sounds splendiferous.

ASH-   Shall we say seven o'clock? ...and please, Julian, call me Karen.

BASHIR- Seven it is, Karen.

Ensign Karen Ash exits.

BASHIR- Gentlemen! What can I do for you? (More solemn) Is there any word on the sabotage?

ODO-   Perhaps.

WORF- We want you to tell us everything you know about the Klingon, K'Lonth Bidar, Doctor!

BASHIR- Err- everything!?

ODO-   Doctor Bashir, as you will have undoubtedly heard, Miss Bidar is the prime suspect in our murder investigation, so any information which you have about her whereabouts this morning would be appreciated.

BASHIR- Err- yes, of course, Constable. (He looks at the glowering Worf.) Miss Bidar was err- with me until err- that is to say, I received your call about the murder at the docking bay at five-thirty...

WORF- Had you consumed any alcohol?

BASHIR- Oh, yes! As it happens, I did... Romulan ale. Potent stuff it was, too!

ODO-   So you parted company at five-thirty?

BASHIR- That's err- corr3ct, yes, Constable.

WORF- Is it possible that she left your room during the night without your knowledge?

BASHIR- (after consideration) Well yes, I suppose she could quite easily have done so. I had to admit it, but Romulan ale always knocks me out for the night, especially this time...I mean err- after how much I consumed.

ODO-   Doctor! Is it possible you left your room without knowing it?

BASHIR- (laughing) I'm not in the habit of walking in my sleep, Constable Odo.

WORF- What did you and...K'Lonth Bidar talk about? Might she have mentioned something about her business here on the station? Something out of context, perhaps?

BASHIR- Not that I recall. In fact, all she really wanted to talk about was me and work...and I was happy to oblige. Oh, and she did ask about Quark's.

ODO-   Indeed?

BASHIR- Yes. She err- Miss Bidar liked the bar. That's where we first met. Oh, ayes, she did mention how well organised the Federation is...and she wasn't being sarcastic. I don't think Klingon's know sarcasm...no offence, Worf. Apparently she pities the Klingon bureaucrats who ended the peace treaty with us.

ODO-   Fascinating!

WORF-   Did K'Lonth Bidar arrange to meet with you later, Doctor?

BASHIR- Err- no, Commander. That's why I agreed to meet Karen err- Ensign Ash first a drink this evening. I wouldn't want to double date a Klingon!

WORF-   A wise decision, Doctor!

ODO-   Did Miss Bidar tell you when she planned to depart Deep Space Nine, Doctor?

BASHIR- No, Constable. When I was called away this morning, we parted with nothing more than a smile, I'm sorry to say.

WORF-   She is a disgrace to the Empire!

BASHIR- I err- won't take that a person insult, Commander.

Worf growled.

ODO-   If you think of anything further, Doctor, you will let us know.

BASHIR- Yes, Constable, of course. I'm only too willing to help.

Worf and Odo exit.

7   Interior Corridor.

Odo and Worf stride away from the Infirmary.

WORF-   The Doctor was not very helpful!

ODO-   On the contrary, Commander. I found Doctor Bashir's answers to be very insightful. Now we know that it had been possible for Miss Bidar to leave the Doctor's room without his knowledge.

WORF-   Why don't we just access the computer security log entry for people entering the Doctor's room? That would give us our second piece of evidence against K'Lonth Bidar…the first being our witness.

ODO-   We already have computer evidence.

Worf stops in his tracks. Odo a stride later.

ODO-   Is there a problem, Commander?

WORF-   Captain Sisko asked that we work together on this investigation, Constable Odo! He believed that with our suspect being a Klingon, and the present unrest between my people and the

Federation, that it would be an advantage for us to join forces! The Captain was conscious of the big picture! What if the sabotage of the Virbitin ship is part of a broader scheme?

ODO- I am well aware of the details, Commander, I was there! What...is...your point?

WORF- My point is, Constable Odo, that you are supposed to divulge all relevant information regarding this case with me, as I would to you! So why was I not made aware that you have already checked computer records.

ODO- There is a simple answer to that, Commander. I am chief of security for this station and have been for many years. I have discretionary duties with how I proceed with an investigation, which includes accounting for all conceivable scenarios. I must be aware of all present threat situations, so as to protect this station to the best of my capacity.

WORF- I do not need a lecture on security protocol, Constable! If you will recall, I was chief of security on the Starship Enterprise for almost seven years! What...are you driving at?

ODO- Commander Worf, let me take you back to your arrival at Deep Space Nine. At that time you were undecided about whether to remain in Starfleet...or pursue a career elsewhere. To me, that seems like a conflict of interest. Although I have come to respect your judgement, there is still the niggling doubt that you may be a very well placed spy for the Klingon Empire!

WORF- That is a ridiculous suggestion!

ODO- Is it? Our prime suspect in this investigation is a Klingon, one whom you have prior acquaintance.

WORF- K'Lonth Bidar had a mutual bonding many years ago, Constable! I cannot see what that could possibly have to do with questioning my own loyalty to Starfleet! Unless you are implying I am somehow involved in this sabotage? Perhaps you believe I murdered Major Kira with aims at eventually killing all senior staff!

ODO- A distinct possibility, Commander!

WORF- Then if that is the case it is I who should be weary of you, Constable Odo! The Founders have infiltrated many key areas of the Federation! Is it not possible you could be one of them?

ODO- It could be, Commander!

They stand in silence for a moment, then continue walking as if nothing has occurred.

WORF- So you have discovered that K'Lonth Bidar did leave Doctor Bashir's quarters this morning?

ODO-   She left at fifteen minutes before oh-five-hundred hours.

WORF-   Hmm- And what is our next step?

ODO-   Firstly, Commander, we shall pay our eye witness a surprise visit…and then we shall find out what Quark knows.

FADE OUT.

ACT TWO:

8   Interior Ops.

O'Brien sighs audibly before stretching backward in his seat at the control table. Dax is tapping out a few commands.

O'BRIEN-   Why the hell is there not a shred of debris? There's not even residual traces of the explosion! I know we know very little about Virbitin technology, but surely if there was an internal explosion aboard their ship, there should be some traces of it! And what about Major Kira's runabout? Nothing!

DAX-   Perhaps when the Virbitin ship's engines exploded the ejection of matter caused everything to simply vaporise?

O'BRIEN-   Replay the reverse and for me again, could you.

Dad's fingers dart along the controls.

9   Exterior DS9 viewing screen.

The image displays docking pylon three from the reverse view we saw early, as the explosion from the Virbitin ship envelops the runabout.

O'BRIEN-   (voice over) In slow motion.

The image repeats at a quarter speed.

10   Interior Ops.

O'BRIEN-   Did you see the runabout actually explode?

Dax taps out some commands.

DAX-   Perhaps there was some kind of Quantum distortion in the system?

O'BRIEN-   So the runabout might have been sent to an alternate dimension when the explosion occurred? Like a time jump of some sort.

DAX-   Computer…at oh-five-hundred this morning were there any reports of a distortion in the space/time continuum near Deep Space Nine, or in the Bajoran system?

COMPUTER- There are no such recorded anomalies.

O'BRIEN- Well, it was worth a try.

DAX- Yes…but it can only mean one thing…

O'BRIEN- Major Kira is definitely dead!

11 Interior Runabout.

The Virbitin male known as Dre sits proudly in the pilots chair studying the controls. He glances up at the viewing screen in front of him, strumming his fingers impatiently on the arm of the chair.

In the rear of the runabout is slumped the unconscious Major Kira. Her wrists and ankles are bound. Her eyes flutter open and she blinks in her surroundings, settling upon Dre.

KIRA- Smoke-Man!

Dre swivels one-eighty degrees in the chair.

DRE- (smiling) My sweet and lovely Bajoran, call me Dre. The name you describe me is a blatant insult. Smoke on my world is a vile substance, while man is an extremely sexist word! I…Dre…am an esteemed officer of the Virbitin elite security council.

KIRA-   What you want, Smoke-Man?

DRE-   Such a sweet voice you have, for someone so lovely! I know you have broken a many heart!

KIRA-   And my fists have broken many a jaw! (contemplative) The last thing I remember was your ship coming at me from the docking pylon...then a transporter activation...before I lost consciousness!

DRE-   (heroic laugh) Yes, that was indeed I! Saving your precious and lovely countenance from the clutches of death!

KIRA-   Don't be too enthusiastic about yourself! I'm not grateful at being held against my will!

DRE-   Regretfully, I have no choice, and I offer my sincere apology! The evil-doer conspiring against me is still hiding aboard your station...and would definitely launch another attack against me should I reveal myself.

KIRA-   How long was I unconscious for?

DRE-   Ten of your hours.

KIRA-   Funny that my people haven't located me yet.

DRE-   Alas, my dear, they have long given up. In fact they are probably mourning your very passing as we speak.

Dre stands, striding across the interior before kneeling in front of Kira.

DRE-   You see, my dear, we are under cloak... and I don't mean one if these inferior Romulan devices, no...I am using something which is far superior! It has been created by the brightest Virbitin minds.

Kira frowns doubtfully.

DRE-   (laughs) Okay, so it was purloined from a source in the Gamma Quadrant!

KIRA-   Why would someone want to murder a mindless oaf like you?

DRE-   I am no oaf, my dear! On my home-world I am an adventurer, a warrior and gallant hero to the people!

KIRA-   And an exaggerator of the truth?

DRE-   Oh no, I'm truly a hero. And the fiend who attempted to murder me was a Klingon warrior, no less! She could not outwit me even with her best laid plan!

KIRA-   Her? So she is a jealous wife!

DRE-   No, no, no...she is a devious mind!

KIRA-   With all due respect, I don't know of many Klingon's that don't possess a devious mind!

DRE-   This particular Klingon is a murderous thief! She stole a sacred crystal belonging to the esteemed Virbitin science council...but using my own cunning ingenuity...

KIRA-   And modesty!

DRE-   ...I tracked her to your space station.

KIRA-   What a hero!

DRE-   You mock me, my dear! This Klingon did her best to elude me for quite some time! In fact...it is my belief that she works for a third party. And alas it is very possible that she has already sold the crystal.

KIRA-   How did you trace her to Deep Space Nine?

DRE-   Ah...more technological wonders procured from the Gamma Quadrant! I had been able to track her very DNA signature. Thankfully that same technology means I know she is still onboard your space station.

KIRA-   This is all very fascinating...but how do I know it's the truth?

DRE- Well I- (shakes his head) No, no, no... once again you are baiting me! Never mind. I was hoping you might be willing and me in my quest... but alas I can see that I was mistaken! Pity. I shall now be forced to eliminate you.

KIRA- You empty threats don't frighten me, Smoke-Man, so don't bother wasting your time!

DRE- (sheepish) Okay, okay, I could never lower myself to harm you...but please...Will you help me? I must confess that some of you ship's controls are...baffling!

KIRA- Get on you knees and grovel!

Dre appears disgusted by the notice until he eventually acquiesces.

DRE- Forgive my shameful ignorance over scientific matters...but that ignorance does not hamper my intellect.

KIRA- Which controls can't you work?

DRE- Ah...to be honest...all of them.

Kira laughs.

DRE- Go ahead...laugh at me...mock my naivety. I am an adventurer, a warrior, and a gallant her of the people of Virbitin. I know how to operate the controls of my own ship! I was shown how to use the cloaking device and scanning inhibitor…(he taps a device on his chest)…but everything else is a mystery to me!

KIRA- Okay, so how do you know this Klingon murderer hasn't somehow nullified your DNA tracker and flown off if a departing freighter?

Dre gestures to the viewing window.

DRE- This window presents a clear view of the majority of your space station!

Kira laughs.

DRE- Please. Will you help me?

KIRA- What exactly do you want me to do?

DRE- I would like…if possible…to be able to scan your space station. The crystal emits a distinctive energy signature…which I can detect on another device from my home-world. If it were possible to lock onto that energy signature…

KIRA- I get the picture. Do you believe it was this Klingon who destroyed your ship?

DRE- Most assuredly.

KIRA- Then perhaps if Constable Odo thinks you are were murdered, rather than the explosion being an accident, he might very well have an ongoing investigation under way...and...knowing Odo...he probably has a few suspects in for questioning.

DRE- What are you suggesting?

KIRA- (rolling her eyes) If Odo has suspects then one of those is most likely this Klingon you've been talking about!

DRE- And how do we find out this information?

KIRA- By accessing the station's security computer.

DRE- How...? No, no, no...don't tell me...you could perhaps access the computer from here?

KIRA- You catch on slowly, Smoke-Man!

DRE- Please...call me Dre.

KIRA- If you release these bonds I will try and you...Dre.

Dre leans forward as if to do her bidding, then reconsiders.

DRE- Wait a moment. I'm not stupid. How do I know that I can trust you?

KIRA- Do you have another option, Dre?

Dre shakes his head. He unties Kira's bonds.

DRE-   I apologise again. I hope your wrists don't hurt. I was as gentle as I could be.

KIRA-   That's not at all creepy…I've experienced worse.

Kira slowly goes to nearest console, showing Dre that she is no threat, who is close behind. Kira taps out a few commands.

KIRA-   Nothing. Your cloaking device not only shields us from them, it's preventing me from externally accessing the station. Is there any way you can lower your cloak…even partially…so I might have a window to operate through?

DRE-   I cannot do that…sorry, my dear.

KIRA-   In that case…there is absolutely nothing I am able to do to help you here.

Dre hangs his head despondently.

KIRA-   Look, Sm…Dre. Captain Sisko is an understanding and compassionate man. I'm sure if you explained your situation to him…exactly like you have to me…then he would be willing to offer all the assistance he can.

DRE-   But…I have abducted you!

KIRA-   Hey, look...if there's a murderer aboard his space station...Captain Sisko is gonna want to know about it! You are the only one who can warn him!

DRE-   Let me consider your proposal.

KIRA-   Of course...just don't take too long...who knows what the Klingon might be plotting right now!

FADE OUT

ACT THREE:

12 Interior Quark's Bar.

Worf and Odo enter the nearly deserted bar.

WORF-   ...and you really believe the Bajoran witness is linked to the murder victim?

ODO-   If there is one thing I have learned about Bajoran's, it is that they normally work in a group. This is too much of a coincidence...and he is just another suspect.

Quark pops his head up from behind the bar. Rom is polishing glass.

ODO-   (under breath) Speaking of which...

QUARK- Isn't this a coincidence! Not moments ago I was asking Rom why we weren't busy! Now I understand the reason...all of my potential customers foresaw the arrival of our two illustrious law enforcers!

ODO- Which implies there are illegal activities present!

QUARK- Not here, my dear Odo! Commander Worf. What can I do to assist you both? Oh! Let me guess...because there has been a murder on docking pylon three...mix that with sabotage...you thought it time to question your usual suspect! Perhaps you even think it was I who killed Major Kira?

ODO- Did you, Quark?

QUARK- As if! The Major was my only reason for staying on this forsaken space station in the first place!...and besides, I have not broken one of you many dubious laws in...days!

WORF- There has been a Klingon female in here! She is quite...eye catching! You know the one I am talking about, Quark!

QUARK- Excuse me, Commander Worf...are you telling me or asking me!?

ROM- (to Quark) Brother...was she the one who sold you that piece of jewellery? She was very... eye-catching even with clothes on!

Quark strikes out at Rom, but Rom blocks with his forearm before sweeping Quark onto the floor.

QUARK- (stunned) You…how…?

ROM- Sorry brother.

Quark pulls himself up, straightens his coat.

QUARK- How dare you! This is an insult! Where did you learn such…hooliganism!?

WORF- (growls) Self defence is not…hooliganism!

QUARK- You taught my brother…self defence?

ODO- Quark!

Quark's attention is redirected.

ODO- Try to pull that little mind back to the issue at hand! Unless that fall has incapacitated you! I need to know what it is the Klingon female sold you.

QUARK- It was nothing of value…just a small piece of jewellery…(at Rom)…utterly worthless!

WORF- If it has no value, Quark, why did you purchase it from her?

QUARK- When I say that it is worthless...I mean it would not of any value to someone like yourself. For me...it is a gift for Moogie...my mother.

ODO-   Didn't you mother die recently?

QUARK- No, no...don't be so idiotic, Constable! Why would I purchase a gift for Moogie if she is dead!?

WORF-   Did the woman tell you the origin of the jewellery...and how she obtained it?

QUARK- No, Commander. I did not ask. I consider that sort of information to be the sellers private business.

ODO-   May we see, Quark?

QUARK- Not unless your eyesight is better than warp speed, Constable. I have already dispatched it to Moogie.

ODO-   Did the seller imply any nefarious reason as to how she initially acquired the piece?

Quark looks baffled.

ODO-   Was it stolen?

QUARK- (shocked) Do you believe that I would knowingly buy my mother a gift that was stolen?

ODO- Yes! (exasperated) You are tediously predictable, Quark. I would have presumed that by now you would have realised that anything you say...anything at all...which pleads your innocence...Will not be taken seriously!

QUARK- Constable Odo...Commander Worf...it would not please me more to help you! If that were possible! But I purchased the item of jewellery in good faith. Honestly. This is the truth and...I know in the past the truth has been flexible between us... but I swear it upon my brothers life!

Rom looks nervous, like he is about to die suddenly.

ODO- I find myself in an unfamiliar situation, Quark. (to Worf) I think I might believe him.

WORF- This does not aid our investigation, Constable! That is unless K'Lonth Bidar is both a saboteur and a murderer! Maybe the pilot of the Virbitin ship was one of her...unfortunate customers?

QUARK- You think that Major Kira was killed by the Klingon female?

ODO- Don't act so surprised, Quark. I don't doubt that you are as much aware of our investigations as we are! (to Worf) Maybe the jewellery offers us her motive?

WORF- It is a shame the pilot of the Virbitin ship did not live! Maybe he could shed some light on the situation.

ODO- We had better report our findings to Captain Sisko.

QUARK- I might be able to save you two fellows some time!

ODO- At a price!

QUARK- On the house! Captain Sisko is in the house! He is using Holo-Suite One.

ODO- Thank you, Quark. That's one I do not owe you!

Odo and Worf walk away from Quark and Rom. Quark turns to his brother.

QUARK- I assume you are befriending Commander Worf for some financial gain which I cannot fathom?

ROM- No, brother. Commander Worf is teaching me self defence!

QUARK- If you value your family…brother…I suggest you don't practice on me again!

ROM- Of course not, brother.

13 Interior Detention Cell.

K'Lonth Bidar is pacing the floor. She stops and nods to herself.

Pulling open the front of her glittery tunic she selects a decorative item of jewellery. She prizes a palm-sized crystal from its encasement.

She stands near the invisible security energy barrier, places the crystal in its path and the energy barrier is absorbed into it.

14 Exterior Baseball Diamond. Day.

Captain Sisko stands at bat. The pitcher winds up before the throw, releasing the ball which Sisko tits with a satisfyingly clunk.

An entrance opens in the Holo-Suite and the ball vanishes in the space as the door opens.

Worf and Odo enter the field.

SISKO-   That was going for a home run!

The comm. beeps.

COMPUTER- Constable Odo to the detention cells. Prisoner is breaking out.

Worf and Odo exchange a brief glance before hurriedly leaving the field. Sisko follows.

SISKO-   End program!

15   Interior Corridor Outside Detention Facility

Worf and Odo clatter past the entrance with Sisko following.

SISKO-   (shout) You think this woman is a thief and saboteur?

ODO-   Yes, Captain! Quark claims to have purchased…an item of jewellery from her! I suspect it was originally stolen!

SISKO-   Meaning her motive for murdering the Bajoran was…?

ODO-   …For something he possessed!

The corridor branches into two. Worf takes one direction, Sisko follows Odo along the other.

SISKO-   (into Comm.) Dax! Have you located the passage of the Klingon fugitive for us yet?

16   Interior Ops.

Dad's fingers dance over her console.

DAX-   (into Comm.) Nothing yet, Captain! Scanning the corridor! One life-form detected ahead of Worf! Wait!

SISKO- (voice only) What is it, Dax!?

DAX- I've just lost the signal, Captain!

17 Odo and Sisko turn tail back the way they came.

SISKO- (into Comm.) Sisko to Worf!

WORF- (voice only) a Worf here, sir!

SISKO- Dax just lost a life-sign directly ahead of you! Use caution! The Constable and I are on our way!

WORF- (voice only) Aye, Captain!

18 Interior Ops.

O'Brien's face fun of surprise.

O'BRIEN- This can't be right!

Dax gives him a quizzical glance.

O'BRIEN- Computer! Show me docking pylon three!

19 Exterior - Space - Docking Pylon Three

A runabout shimmers into existence.

20 Interior Ops.

O'BRIEN-   This is impossible!

Dax has a broad smile on her face.

O'BRIEN-   There are no traces of tachyon particles!

DAX-   At least we know we're not being invaded by Romulans, Chief.

O'BRIEN-   We're being hailed!

KIRA-   (voice only) Permission to come aboard, Chief O'Brien!

O'BRIEN-   Permission granted!

21 Interior Runabout.

Dre watches Kira with unconcealed admiration as she deftly operates the guidance controls.

KIRA-   (into Comm.) I have the pilot of the Virbitin ship with me, Chief! He needs to talk to Captain Sisko about the murderer loose on DS9!

DAX-   (voice only) A Klingon by the name of K'Lonth Bidar, Major?

KIRA-   The same!

DRE-   Do they have her?

KIRA-   I think we're about to find out.

22 Interior Corridor.

A panel, low in the wall, hangs loose.

Worf scans the damage with his tricorder.

Sisko and Odo join him.

ODO-   What's happened, Commander?

WORF-   This panel has been forcibly removed, Constable. This was obviously a concealed compartment! Bidar was here only a short time ago. I'm showing traces of a weapons signature.

ODO-   She's armed herself!

SISKO- But how is she able to disappear from sensors!?

WORF-   A personal cloaking device!

The Comm. beeps.

DAX-   (voice only) Dax to Sisko!

SISKO- Go ahead.

DAX-   (voice only) Major Kira us alive, Benjamin! She's with the pilot of the Virbitin ship! They're on their way to you!

SISKO- Acknowledged! (to Worf and Odo) now what!?

WORF- Hopefully the pilot can tell us what Bidar is after!

ODO- And maybe his to find her!?

FADE OUT.

ACT FOUR:

23 Interior Ops.

O'Brien is checking a computer readout. Dax is with him.

O'BRIEN- The has to be a residual trace from the cloaking device! Even the smallest hint of tachyons! But…nothing!

DAX- Maybe the Klingon has a cloaking device similar to the Jem'Hadar?

O'BRIEN- Perhaps she is Jem'Hadar!

DAX- But Chief…we ran all the standard DNA tests when she came aboard. Shes a Klingon as far as the computers concerned.

O'BRIEN- That might be so…but it's been done before! Although that time was before security was increased because of possible Dominion infiltration.

24 Interior Corridor.

Kira and Dre are exiting a station lift in front if the waiting Sisko, Worf and Odo.

SISKO-   It's good to have you amongst the living again, Major.

KIRA-   It's good to be alive!

DRE-   Captain Sisko! It's a pleasure to meet you!

Dre pumps Sisko's hand enthusiastically.

DRE-   It was unfortunate that you were always too busy to meet with before I left the station!

SISKO- Let's make up for missed opportunities now, shall we…?

DRE-   Call me Dre. I'm an officer of the Virbitin security council, an adventurer, warrior, and hero of the people!

KIRA-   That's not a boast, Captain! I think it's Dre's standard greeting!

SISKO- I see…welcome aboard. Now…what happened to your ship?

DRE-   It was sabotaged!

WORF-   (mutter) No kidding!

DAX-   (voice only) Ops to Captain Sisko.

SISKO- Go ahead!

DAX-   (voice only) Chief O'Brien and I have concluded the Klingon has a personal cloaking device...using identical technology to the Jem'Hadar...and that which concealed Major Kira's runabout.

SISKO- Thank you, old man. We already reached that conclusion ourselves. We will head to the Constable's office to review footage of her escape. Keep me posted.

DAX-   (voice only) Aye, Captain.

SISKO- (to Dre) So K'Lonth Bidar sabotaged your ship. Why would she want you dead?

DRE-   She stole something from my homeworld.

ODO-   And what if the dead Bajoran, Mister Dre?

DRE-   I don't know anything about a dead... Bajoran...no. Maybe he got in K'Lonth's way?

25 Interior Constable Odo's Office.

Odo is seated behind his desk. Sisko, Worf, Kira and Dre are standing opposite.

Odo operates a few touch controls and footage from K'Lonth's prison break is show on the monitor before them.

DRE- She still has it! (gleeful pointing) There!

ODO- What...Mister Dre...does she still have?

DRE- The Xloxic power crystal, of course!

WORF- What does a...Xloxic power crystal do?

DRE- It...has the potential to wreak havoc on this station! Captain Sisko, part of me is very happy to see that it is still in her possession...yet I am also fearful. We have to retrieve it from her immediately! It should be back in the hands of our strategic military division.

KIRA- On the runabout you told me it belongs to your science council!

DRE- Well, yes, I...

ODO- What makes this crystal such a potent weapon?

DRE- (nervous laugh) To be honest with you... all of you...I have no idea what its capabilities are!

You see…I'm not a scientist! All I know…all I have been told…is that the Xloxic crystal is a powerful and dangerous weapon in the wrong hands.

SISKO- Are weapons really any other way…even in the right hands!?

WORF- I think this entire story is fiction!!

DRE- I appreciate that it seems this way…but… I must return the crystal to my home otherwise…my career…and family name….will be sullied for generations to come! I shall no longer be an adventurer, a warrior, and hero to my people!(to Sisko) Captain…I know nothing about the moral implications of such a devastating weapon…but I do know that I must return it!

ODO- This isn't getting us very far! We have a dangerous fugitive onboard…and I need to know everything you can tell us about her modus operandi!

DRE- Her…what?

ODO- The way she operates!

DRE- (nervous) I must admit…and I'm truly sorry…I should have been honest with right away… but I know nothing of her methods!

KIRA- But you said you'd been tracking K'Lonth Bidar using some DNA device!

WORF- And you have a cloaking device similar to her own!

DRE- This will be my…second encounter with the Klingon woman!

KIRA- The standard of hero on your world must be real low!

DRE- I'm…what's the word…sorry?

SISKO- We have to locate the Klingon fugitive before she has time to leave Deep Space Nine…or worse! I need suggestions!

KIRA- Couldn't we utilise the Smoke-Man's cloaking device somehow? Perhaps if we could expand its range it might reveal her whereabouts?

DRE- It has limited range!

WORF- Do you suppose Chief O'Brien could isolate its frequency?

SISKO- It's worth a try, Commander!

DRE- I could…activate my cloak…if it operates on the same range as hers…I could find her!

WORF- What's to prevent you from running! You've already attended it once!

ODO- And say we went with your idea…how would we be able to track you?

DRE- I…

SISKO- Is there some way we could modulate a comm. badge so its signal was traceable through the cloak?

Odo tosses a comm. badge to Dre.

ODO- Do not leave this room until I have a signal lock! I won't hesitate to shoot if that door opens by itself! Now…activate your cloak.

Dre vanishes.

Odo brushes his hand on the console until successful.

ODO- It's working!

SISKO- Mister Dre! I want no heroics! Is that understood!?

DRE- (voice only) Yes, Captain Sisko. You have my word.

SISKO- Then please proceed.

The opens by itself, then closes seconds later.

KIRA- What happens if Dre finds her?

SISKO- (into comm. badge) Sisko to Ops.

26 Interior Ops.

DAX- Dax here, sir.

SISKO- I need Odo's comm. badge tracked!

O'BRIEN- On it! Sir! I'm also detecting an unauthorised transport signature from cargo bay four to the promenade!

27 Interior Constable Odo's Office.

Worf dashes to the door.

SISKO- (into comm.) Acknowledged, Chief! (to Odo) I want you in cargo bay four…just in case the transport is a decoy!

Sisko and Kira follow Work out of the office at a run, while…

ODO- (into comm.) Odo to Ops. Site to site transport to cargo bay four. Now!

28 Interior Upper Promenade.

POV K'Lonth Bidar as she looks upon the entrance to Quark's Bar.

29 Interior Cargo Bay Four.

Odo materialises just inside that bay door. A Starfleet Officer is laying on the floor near the transporter pad. Odo slaps a comm. panel beside the door.

ODO- (into comm.) Medical team to cargo bay four!

Odo leans down to the injured Officer, whose eyes are open but she is in great pain.

ODO- What happened here?

OFFICER- I was…transferring components to a storage locker when…I heard something fall… over there…and when I investigated I was jumped by a…a Klingon woman!

ODO- Hmm…who led back here to the transporter so she wouldn't prematurely trip any alarms. Very clever!

Odo looks across at the pad…an object is laying on the floor close by…it emits a high-pitched whine before exploding.

30 Interior Corridor and Entrance of Quark's Bar

We look out at the empty corridor.

K'Lonth Bidar is standing outside.

Dre rounds a corner. Bidar sees him.

Sisko, Worf and Kira follow.

Dre points at Bidar.

POV Sisko. Dre and Bidar are not visible.

DRE-   (voice only) She is outside the bar! Wait! No! She just went inside!

31 Interior Quark's Bar.

Bashir holds two drinks. He nods a thank you to Quark behind the bar, before turning to the room and looks across to his table where Karen Ash is seated.

Bashir's drinks fly dramatically from his hands, and he is abruptly wrenched to one side.

Sisko, Worf and Kira enter, weapons drawn.

DRE-   (voice only) She has a knife at his throat!

SISKO-   Doctor! Don't move!

Bashir struggles with an invisible force.

BASHIR- Who has a knife at my throat?

Bidar abruptly de-cloaks. She has a Kingon d'k tahg at Bashir's throat. Quark ducks out of sight. Bar patrons have cowered to the far side of the room. Bidar throws Bashir's comm. badge away.

BIDAR- Sorry, Doctor! (to Sisko et al) Don't come any closer! And tell that Virbitin gagh-excrement to lower his cloak, otherwise the good doctor here will find that he is his own next patient!

SISKO- Dre! Do as she says!

Dre de-cloaks behind Worf.

Bidar and Kira laugh at him.

BIDAR- (to Dre) You are nothing but a snivelling excuse of your species! Hiding by a real warrior!

DRE- I...I...simply did not wish to provoke you!

BASHIR- (to Bidar) I...assume this isn't because of me?

BIDAR- Not at all, Doctor...you were amazing... for a human! I'm sorry you were chosen as my... hostage...you were in the wrong place...

BASHIR- ...at the wrong time. Yes, I see that now.

BIDAR- (to Sisko) Please tell your people to back up, Captain! I need...room to move!

Sisko nods to his officers, and they make a clear passage to the entrance.

Bidar slowly makes her way with Bashir's at knife point toward the entrance.

BIDAR- (to Dre) Better luck next time! (to Sisko) Nobody is to follow us!

SISKO- (exasperated sigh) I know how this works! And it tires me to say that you will not leave this station!

BIDAR- That remains to be seen!

SISKO- You really have nowhere to go.

BIDAR- That remains to be seen, Captain.

Bidar shoves Bashir along the corridor in front of her, until they are both out of sight.

SISKO- (into comm.) Sisko to Ops. Can you please track K'Lonth Bidar and Doctor Bashir! Do not attempt any beam out!

DAX- (voice only) Understood.

SISKO- Anything yet from Odo?

DAX- (voice only) No, sir.

SISKO-   (to Dre) I need you cloaked and to follow them! We shall be as close behind as we dare risk. Understood?

DRE-   Aye, aye, Captain.

Dre cloaks himself.

KIRA-   Captain! What is the Klingon woman's angle? Why didn't she simply run while the Smoke-Man was the only one who could see her?

WORF- Maybe we have underestimated her. Perhaps she has unfinished business to attend to! Odo was convinced that the eye-witness we have to the murder on docking pylon three was involved more than he was saying.

SISKO-   Oh?

WORF- Both the eye witness and the murder victim are Bajoran.

KIRA-   Odo thinks it's some kind of vendetta?

WORF- Or maybe the K'Lonth Bidar is a hired assassin!

SISKO-   Then…who hired her?

FADE OUT.

ACT FIVE:

32 Interior Promenade Branch Corridor.

Bashir is laying unconscious on the ground.

Sisko, Worf and Kira are with him.

SISKO-   Stay with Dre!

Worf and Kira leave.

DAX-   (voice only) Dax to Sisko. The fugitive has released Doctor Bashir and is on her own!

SISKO-   Thank you, old man! Can you send a med team to my location? (on comm. to Dre) Get moving, Dre! She's on her own!

Bashir stirs. Pain creases his face.

SISKO-   Don't worry Doctor…help is on its way.

34 Interior Corridor.

Worf and Kira are jogging along the length of the corridor.

KIRA-   Where's the Smoke-Man?

WORF-   Twenty metres ahead!

KIRA-   (on comm.) Any signs of her, Smoke-Man?

DRE-   (voice only) Not yet, my dear.

A door opens a pace in front of Kira. A second later Kira writhes to floor in pain, blood on her hand clutched to her side.

KIRA-   It's her!

Worf growls, charges forward blindly and crashes into the cloaked Bidar, who crackles into existence. Bidar strikes with her d'k tahg, Worf blocks hard and the blade clatters to the deck.

Dre de-cloaks.

Bidar knocks Work to the deck, straddling him. Worf thrown her over his shoulders.

Dre cowers.

Bidar and Worf are soon to their feet. Sisko appears from around the corridor corner.

WORF-   You won't…be wanting…(he opens his hand)…this!

Bidar glowers at the object in his hand: her portable cloaking device.

BIDAR- You still have remarkable reflexes, Worf. But so have I.

In a flash, Bidar draws out her phaser and shoots at Dre, who dissolves. She turns it on Worf but Sisko fires first. Bidar dissolves.

SISKO- (to Worf) Well done, Commander.

WORF- She had little honour, Captain!

SISKO- (to comm.) Sisko to ops! Beam Major Kira directly to the infirmary!

KIRA- They're a bit stretched…today!

35 Interior Cargo Bay Four.

The area around the transporter pad is blackened from the explosion. O'Brien is scanning the pad with his tricorder. Sisko and Worf enter.

SISKO- Report, Chief!

O'BRIEN- The explosive was tetra-alpha-diosiphide, sir. About a quarter kilo of the stuff! Lucky it was contained here! Who knows what damage it might've caused in a more sensitive area.

WORF- Was there enough to kill Constable Odo?

O'BRIEN- I'm sorry to say…yes. I've not found a trace of him.

Sisko thumps the wall.

SISKO- What next!

36 Interior Infirmary.

Kira lays prostrate on a medical bed, wired up to various equipment. She is unconscious.

Bashir has a wistful smile on his face as he faces Karen Ash by the doorway.

ASH- Do you stand up all your dates!?

BASHIR- I…I'm sorry, Karen, it's been…

ASH- I'm teasing you, Julian! I realise there was nothing you could do. I just wanted to make sure that you are all right?

BASHIR- Er…yes…I er…I'm fine. Thank you.

ASH- That's good to hear, Julian. I was worried the Klingon woman was going to hurt you! What time…do you think you'll be free today?

BASHIR- Er…soon…maybe another hour.

ASH- Dinner in an hour and half, then! But not at Quark's…I've gone off the bar…that's too risky! I will prepare something for you in my quarters.

BASHIR- That er…that sounds perfect.

37 Interior Runabout.

A Bajoran sits at the pilots controls.

PILOT- (to comm.) This is runabout Trinidad requesting permission to depart for Bajor.

38 Interior Ops.

Dax sits at the control console.

DAX- Stand by. (to comm.) Ops to Captain Sisko.

SISKO- (voice only) Go ahead.

DAX- Runabout Trinidad is requesting permission to depart for Bajor, Benjamin. The pilot is our eye-witness.

39 Interior Cargo Bay Four.

Sisko looks to Worf.

WORF- We have no more use for the witness now that K'Lonth Bidar and Dre are dead, Captain.

Sisko nods.

SISKO- (to comm.) Let up go, Dax.

DAX- (voice only) Aye, aye, Captain!

SISKO- All these senseless killing for a weapon that is now of no use to anyone!…and Constable Odo is dead because two people brought their own issues onto this station! I realise I should expect anything by now…but it's still hard to swallow when an officer of mine is killed!

WORF- Constable Odo died with honour, sir!

Sisko nods reluctantly.

40 Interior Runabout.

The Bajoran pilot looks over the controls. A reflection from behind distracts him. When he turns, he faces K'Lonth Bidar and Dre, and his face drops.

PILOT- This is…impossible. I heard you were both dead!

BIDAR- Did you stop worrying about me! Did you think you had…escaped my wrath?

DRE- This might be your last time for honesty!

PILOT- I do not know what to say!

DRE- How about you tell us why your friend planted that bomb on my ship?

BIDAR- And why did you sacrifice me to the space station's security chief? We were all supposed to be working together!

PILOT- I...

DRE- Maybe you didn't think we could accomplish this mission? Did you believe us incapable of taking over Deep Space Nine...when the four of us had been friends...for so long!

BIDAR- Answer now...or suffer more pain than you have ever experienced!

The pilots drops his head with shame.

PILOT- (sobbing) I...I'm sorry...

BIDAR- Stop snivelling you excuse for a man! I'm not going to kill you...although I might torture you before our mission is accomplished!

DRE- This set-back has cost us a lot of time... fortunately our employers are renowned for their patience!

The pilot looks up, hope in his eyes, quickly replaced with resignation.

BIDAR- What now...?

Bidar turns her head first, followed by Dre. Behind them is Odo.

DRE- How...?

ODO- Because...I am better prepared than amateurs like you! Although your scheme was... grander than I expected!

BIDAR- Why were you not killed in the explosion I planned?

ODO- Maybe your employer is ill informed! (to comm.) Computer. Return us to DS9!

41 Interior Detention Cells.

K'Lonth Bidar, Dre, and the Bajoran pilot, sit in individual cells. Worf and Odo are present.

ODO- Enjoy your stay gentlemen...lady!

42 Interior Corridor.

Worf and Odo walk at a leisurely pace.

WORF- Are you going to tell me how you realised K'Lonth Bidar and Dre were working together?

ODO- Of course, Commander. The evidence came together a piece at a time...as these things do! Firstly...Dre made a slip-up when he mentioned the murder victim was male...something nobody told him...and the mistake of a novice! Secondly, after Bidar's unsuccessful attack on me...I investigated the store-room where she had constructed a fake cloaking device controller, which she knew would be the first think confiscated! And in your fight with her...she had a phaser set on stun only...which I discovered...plus a personal energy shield of Borg manufactured technology.

WORF- We still do not know who paid these criminals to carry out the scheme to take over Deep Space Nine.

ODO- I suspect it was the Dominion! But I wouldn't put it past the Cardassian. Whoever it was, though...despite causing a bit of harm...they underestimated me and was thus doomed from the start! They will have to try much harder to wrest the station from me!

FADE OUT.

"Don't give up the day job."

Please feel free to email me at:

p.starling@sky.com

with all spelling and grammatical errors, plus your name so that I might acknowledge your assistance in future editions of this work. I self edit my work and, being an imperfect human, there are things I miss.

Thank you for reading this collection, my tenth novel, and one which I have thoroughly had fun with.

The crew of the Sol Ship Excel will return - sorry about that! - in a second volume, which will include the Star Trek Voyager script I submitted to Paramount Pictures during the 1900's.

But most importantly: Don't forget to squeeze the lemon dry…

Printed in Great Britain
by Amazon